Shatter

ADDICTED TO YOU #3

K.M. SCOTT

Books by K.M. Scott

If I Dream (Corrupted Love #1)
If You Fight (Corrupted Love #2)
If We Fall (Corrupted Love #3)

Crash Into Me (Heart of Stone #1)
Fall Into Me (Heart of Stone #2)
Give In To Me (Heart of Stone #3)
Heart of Stone Volume One Box Set
Ever After (Heart of Stone #4)
A Heart of Stone Christmas (Heart of Stone #5)
Unforgettable (Heart of Stone #6)
Unbreakable (Heart of Stone #7)
Heart of Stone Volume Two Box Set

Temptation (Club X #1)
Surrender (Club X #2)
Possession (Club X #3)
Satisfaction (Club X #4)
Acceptance (Club X #5)

Crave (Addicted To You #1)
Adore (Addicted To You #2)
Shatter (Addicted To You #3)
Claim (Addicted To You #4)

Books by K.M. Scott writing as Gabrielle Bisset

Blood Avenged (Sons of Navarus #1)

Blood Betrayed (Sons of Navarus #2)

Longing (A Sons of Navarus Short Story)

Blood Spirit (Sons of Navarus #3)

The Deepest Cut (A Sons of Navarus Short Story)

Blood Prophecy (Sons of Navarus #4)

Blood Craving (Sons of Navarus #5)

Blood Eclipse (Sons of Navarus #6)

The Sons of Navarus Box Set #1

The Sons of Navarus Box Set #2

Stolen Destiny (Destined Ones Duology #1)

Destiny Redeemed (Destined Ones Duology #2)

Love's Master

Masquerade

The Victorian Erotic Romance Trilogy

Shatter is a work of fiction. Names, characters, places, and events are the products of the author's imagination. Any resemblance to events, locations, or persons, living or dead, is coincidental.

2017 Copper Key Media, LLC
Print Edition

Copyright © 2017 Copper Key Media, LLC

Published in the United States

ISBN-10: 1-941594-64-6
ISBN-13: 978-1-941594-64-3

Cover Design: Patricia Maia at Maya's Teasers & Designs

Adult Content: Contains graphic sexual content

For Ian Anwell, addiction is a way of life. He can't remember a time when he wasn't addicted to something—heroin, alcohol, whatever made him feel good. But his newest addiction is better than all the others combined. Kristina makes him feel like the man he's always wanted to be.

But addicts have a habit of wrecking things, even those they hold dear.

For Kristina Richards, Ian is everything. Love. Lust. Obsession. But even as she falls deeper in love with him and the madness they create together, she finds something she never expected to find in her time with him.

She finds strength she never knew she had.

Shatter was previously published as SILK Volume Three.

CHAPTER ONE

Ian

FIVE WEEKS. I haven't seen or heard from Kristina in five weeks. Until this morning as I boarded the plane to return to New York, I would have lied if someone asked me if I still thought about her. I would have said no. Lying would have been easy four thousand miles away in that beautiful city I so looked forward to sharing with her.

Now that I'm back in New York, lying isn't as easy anymore. The minute I stepped off the plane I felt her pull on me. For all that this city has meant in my life, after Kristina it simply reminds me of her.

I look around my apartment and see her. Everything is a memory that tortures me. The couch where we sat together as I read the words that enchanted her. The kitchen where I found joy in making meals just for her. The bed where we lost ourselves in one another. My stomach tightens as I think about us. I can't be here right now.

Dropping my bags, I head out into a November storm that's nothing less than raw. The feel of the cold rain on my face matches my mood. I don't know where I'm going, but I walk fast, making the rain pelt my skin even harder. At some point I realize I'm walking toward Kristina's place and stop dead in the middle of an intersection.

A car screeches to a stop, barely missing me, and the driver screams, "Get the fuck out of the way!"

His words barely register as I try to figure out where to go. I live in a city with practically limitless opportunities to do things, but I don't know where to go or what to do to forget Kristina. For five weeks, I thought I'd gotten over her. I'd lied to myself, aided by the benefit of distance, but I couldn't do that anymore.

Stumbling toward the sidewalk, I hear the guy bark again, "Get your head out of your ass!"

He has no idea how accurate his assessment of me is. I find an awning to get out of the rain as it begins to pour down and watch as a couple madly in love kisses next to me. Their happiness brings a dull ache to my chest, and I turn away, unable to watch them. I wanted Kristina and me to be that happy, but it wasn't meant to be.

I could call her now that I'm back. I could tell her I forgive her for lying to me and letting me leave. But I can't lie that well. Not to her. I can't forgive her either.

That's not true. I could forgive her for lying to me. I've lied for so many years I don't even know the truth about some things anymore, so lying is a sin I can forgive.

Letting me go isn't.

Knowing that she very well might lose me forever if she let me get on that plane alone and still letting it happen I can't forgive. By doing that, she showed she doesn't love me like I love her.

Madly. Completely. As if every breath I take depends on having her in my life.

I was able to lie for five long weeks as I buried myself in research and Marc Antony's life. And drugs. I pretended like I didn't love her more than life itself.

Now I can't anymore.

The couple next to me walks away as I stand there unsure of what to do now that I've admitted the truth to myself. I can't forgive her, but I can't live without her.

The rain begins to slow to a light drizzle, so I head out from underneath the store awning back toward my apartment. I need a drink. I need something else. I know I shouldn't want it, but as I make my way back to my place, that need starts to push out all thoughts of Kristina.

No. As painful as it is to think of her, I can't let my craving for heroin take over. I've just spent five weeks deep in it, but I promised myself once I got back here I'd stop.

My legs break into a run as I desperately try to get home, my breathing creating a cloud in the icy air around me. But as I round the last corner I see it. A picture of her on a magazine cover. She looks incredible. Fresh, soft, feminine. I stop in front of the newsstand, lost in the vision of her, and then I see the words above her head.

ACTRESS KRISTINA RICHARDS IN TORRID LOVE AFFAIR

Five fucking weeks is all we've been apart and she's already involved in some torrid love affair? I can't bear to pick up the rag and flip through the pages to read the details of this incredible love match she's apparently made.

Instead I just stand there staring like some idiot until the man who owns the stand asks me if I need help. Yeah, I need help. I need some way to fucking forget the most important person in my life.

I need help.

I grimace and shake my head before I race back to my apartment, feeling unhappier than I've felt since the last time I entered rehab. By the time I get home, I want some junk so bad my hands are shaking.

Closing the front door, I press my back against it and take a deep breath, just like they taught me to do in rehab. Take a deep breath in and push all those thoughts out of your mind. The desire to feel good again—to feel nothing but pure bliss and not have to endure the pain of knowing Kristina is with someone else—that's what I want. If the only way to get it is snorting shit up my nose, then I'll take it.

Thoughts of how much I want to get high again intermingle with thoughts of how much I miss her. They wrap around my brain like some horrible dream of the perfect pleasure and pain. The feeling of floating peacefully above myself without worry or sadness one minute, pushed aside by the memory of having Kristina in my arms that I know now was all a lie the next.

I slide to the floor and hang my head, silently begging for some relief from the torture of wanting something I shouldn't have and missing someone I can't have. All I want is to forget. That's all I ask.

Why can't I just forget her?

Was she with this torrid love affair guy while she was telling me she loved me? I can't help but wonder.

Jesus, I don't want to be like this. I don't want to feel all this pain.

I struggle to my feet and feel a surge of anger course through me. I hate her. I love her. I need her. I can't stand how much I miss her. I spent five weeks researching Marc Antony and she spent that time fucking another man.

My rage takes over, and I storm across the room toward my desk where all my work for the new historical fiction book sits as a sickening reminder that she let me go. With one swipe of my arm, I send the books and papers flying onto the floor, leaving only my laptop undisturbed. For a moment, I remember the nights when Kristina and I lay in bed as I read her what I'd written and then I have the laptop in my hands ready to throw it.

I don't know how to stop my mind from racing with thoughts about her.

Slowly, I lower the laptop back down to my desk and close my eyes to concentrate on pushing all these thoughts out of my mind. Relax. Breathe. Let your mind release those thoughts and let them go.

I try, but nothing they said would work in rehab seems to be working now. Instead, all this relaxing and breathing is making me wish I had just a little junk to give me peace. That's not good.

Scotch is, though, and if that's what will help me forget Kristina and heroin for at least a little while, then scotch is just what I need. I pour myself a glass and instantly feel my body relax as the scent of the alcohol wafts up toward my nostrils. Good old scotch.

Three hours later, I've welcomed enough of my old friend back into my system that my mind isn't racing anymore. It's barely doing much of anything, but that's better than the alternative. Closing my eyes, I let the scotch slide down my throat and warm my insides as I lean back against my leather couch and look forward to the moment the alcohol knocks me out.

I watch her walk toward me, her dark hair blowing in the cold October wind as she works to push it off her face. Flustered from her attempts to look like what she thinks is beautiful, she's more charming than she even knows. I want to take her in my arms right here on the sidewalk in front of my building and kiss her like she deserves to be kissed.

Long and deep and full of the love I feel for her.

"You didn't have to wait for me in this wind.

It's like a tornado out here!" she says as she fusses with my collar.

I touch her hands. They feel like two blocks of ice. "Let's get upstairs. Your hands are cold."

She gives me a gentle smile. "You're so sweet. Do you have anything planned for us tonight?"

Sliding my tongue across my lips, I smile. "I do. Let's get upstairs so I can show you."

"I wish I could kiss you right here, you know that?" she whispers next to my cheek. "But the minute I do, you just know there will be someone with a camera right behind us."

I look around pretending to scope out any potential paparazzi. "I think we're in the clear. You've been laying low for a few months so the media has moved on to someone who can't keep their dirty laundry private."

Kristina leans away from me and knits her brows unhappily. "I don't consider you dirty laundry, Ian."

"Well, I'm going to have to do something to change that," I say with a grin as I think about all the things I want to do to her as soon as we get upstairs.

"Let's go inside then and you can show me what you have planned."

I take her by the hand and tug her into the lobby of my building as Michael, the doorman, flashes me a knowing smile and gives me a nod. I feel like a *teenager sneaking a girl into my parents' house. It's silly and stupid, but this is the effect she has on me.*

Somehow this gentle soul makes my dark one lighter.

We make out in the elevator, and when the old woman from the floor above me gets on with us, there's no mistaking her look of disgust at our impropriety at kissing in public. Kristina hides her face in the collar of my wool jacket, but Mrs. Jenkins' judgment doesn't affect me. She never liked me anyway.

At least that's how I took her comment that one day that the only history worth any New Yorker's time was American history. As if studying and writing about anything older than the seventeenth century made me some kind of fucking literary criminal.

Crazy old bag.

We get off at my floor, but not before my neighbor shoots us another nasty look for having fun. She's lucky my hands are still cold or she would have gotten a real show since I can't keep them off Kristina.

As we head down my hallway, I say to her, "There's our future, you know that?"

Kristina turns toward me and shakes her head in disbelief. "Like her? I can't imagine either of us so miserable about other people's happiness."

I unlock my front door and nod. "Age does things

to people, I guess. Not that I can ever imagine cranky old Mrs. Jenkins as anything other than the person she is now. She was probably born old and crotchety."

Kristina giggles. "That would be one ugly baby, Ian."

Closing the door, I walk up behind her and slide my hands under her coat as I nuzzle her warm skin. "Enough talk about her. I've got much better things in mind."

"Like what?" she asks with a playful lilt to her voice.

She slips out of her coat, and I hang it up near the door. "I think we'll eat first and then I thought we'd relax. Maybe do a little research for something I want to put into the book."

Kristina gives me a knowing smile, but she has no idea what I mean. As I sat writing this afternoon while the wind blew and the raindrops hit the windows, I had an idea for a scene with Kate that I'm dying to try with my muse.

No woman I've ever known can play the coquette like Kristina, and my announcement about what I have planned for the night brings out the a flirtatiousness only she can carry off with a combination of demure looks and excitement in her soft blue eyes that telegraphs her desire for our time together to begin.

"What's for dinner?"

I trail my fingertip over the swell of her lower lip and suck it gently into my mouth before I pull away and say, "Fuck dinner. Follow me."

Taking her by the hand, I lead her to my bedroom. Of all the times we've been together on all the surfaces of my apartment, there's just one that we've never tried.

The bathroom. More specifically, the sunken bathtub.

I stop in the doorway and hear Kristina's sharp intake of breath as she first sees the bathroom. "I thought the bathroom I always use was impressive. What is this?"

"The couple who lived here before me had a thing for bathrooms. This was a third bedroom at one point, but they turned it into their own personal spa. I don't usually bother with it, but as I was writing this afternoon, I couldn't get the idea of you and me in that tub out of my head."

She steps into the room and slowly spins around trying to take in all the stunning design. I have to admit it's impressive. Black marble mixed with white subway tiles gives the room a sexy look. I may not need a bathroom like this, but I know luxury when I see it. A pristine white marble tub in the center of the room surrounded by a platform gives it a sunken tub feel all the way up here on the fourteenth floor.

Kristina's eyes light up as she spies the shower

area. "Is that a rainfall shower? I saw that in a magazine once and swore I'd have one if I had to make fifty movies to get it."

I slip my arms around her waist and kiss her neck. "Yeah, but the scene I have in my mind takes place in the tub."

Her body melts into mine, and she leans her head back on my shoulder. "Why not both? Then you could choose between them and pick the one that works best."

"I like the way you think."

She turns in my hold and wraps her arms around my neck. "So how does this scene begin?"

Sliding her sweater dress over her head, I step back to admire her matching bra and garter belt. I swipe my tongue over my lips at the sight of Kristina so incredibly sexy and smile. "Just like this."

I unhook the fire engine red silk bra and let it slide to the marble floor, and she seductively removes her tights, garter belt, and red stiletto heels. Standing there in front of me, she's naked and more gorgeous than any woman I've ever seen in my life. My mind begins to fill with ideas that contradict the scene I'd created hours earlier, but that doesn't matter now.

"So now what happens?" she asks shyly. "How does the scene go?"

"I think we should forget all that and make it up as we go along."

Kristina bites her lower lip and smiles as her

hands travel to unzip my fly. "Do you think we can improve on what you envisioned this afternoon? You are the author."

She palms my cock and strokes it as I struggle to control my desire to fuck her right there before we get anywhere close to the tub or the shower. Swallowing hard, I answer, "I think it might turn out to be even better."

"Mmmm…good. Did you happen to see me on my knees and sucking your cock when you thought about this scene?"

My eyes roll back in my head at the mere mention of her mouth on me, and nearly panting, I say, "No, but you see how improvising is making it better already?"

As she lowers herself to the floor, she licks her lips and nods. "Uh huh."

When she looks up at me with those big blue eyes so full of innocence and just a touch of bad girl, I almost come before she even slides her lips down my cock. Some women have that effect on a man, and Kristina is that woman for me.

Without another word, she wraps her hand around the base of my cock and sucks the head into her mouth with a whispersoft touch that makes my knees go weak. Her hand grips me as she strokes over my skin, sending the purest pleasure racing through my body.

It's even better than I'd imagined hours earlier.

It's heaven.

I watch her move her mouth and hand up and down me and for possibly the first time in my life, it's not just about how I physically feel. I know how tentative she still feels with this particular sex act, and still she willingly dropped to her knees to please me.

The memory of that night hurts more now that I know whatever I was feeling was one-sided. It was all an act. She's moved on and all I'm left with is memories and missing her. I can't handle either of them.

I need something to make me forget, and scotch isn't doing it.

CHAPTER TWO

Kristina

THE CABBIE LOVES to chat to his fares, and for one of the few times in my life, I'm thankful for the distraction. Being back in New York brings all the memories of my time with Ian back with a vengeance, making me want to cry at how much I still miss him. I thought all the weeks apart while he was in Rome would help, but the loss of him in my life only gets worse every day I don't see him or hear him say one of those things that always sounded so perfect coming out of his mouth.

"The weather has been nightmarish, even for this city," the cabbie says as he weaves his way through Upper West Side traffic.

Considering it's rush hour, we're making great time, but I'm in no hurry to be back in my apartment. Too many memories there. I'll only be home for four days, and something tells me that will be too long knowing he's just a few blocks away.

"It's still better than Vancouver weather," I say as the cabbie continues to chatter on about the wind and rain the city has been getting pummeled with.

I cradle my signed copy of Caligula's Dream in my lap. Flipping to the page where Ian wrote that I was his greatest fan, I trace my fingertip over his handwriting, so strong and so masculine with its sharp angles and total lack of roundness.

I can't help but remember that first night at my apartment. He didn't know about any of the gossip that I was sure would make him not like me. Nothing about what had happened with John or all the awful things the tabloids had printed about me being so pathetic after he'd left me for that hotel slut.

None of it had mattered to Ian.

My cell phone rings as the cabbie begins to explain what he read in the Farmer's Almanac about how this winter is predicted to be a bad one for the northeast, but even my talking to someone else doesn't stop him from reporting what some groundhog or caterpillar thinks will happen over the next few months.

I answer it and see it's Cilla. "Hey you! Are you back in the Big Apple yet?"

"Hi Cilla. Yeah, I'm home for a few days. Are

you here or in LA?"

She clucks her tongue like she's disgusted about what she's going to say next. "LA. But I should be back there in about a week."

"I'll be gone back to Vancouver by then."

In truth, I'm not really that disappointed I won't be able to see Cilla this week. She's never been very good at empathy, and with how I'm feeling about being back in New York, she'd just give me a hard time about being down. Even worse, she'd push and push to find out what's making me sad, which is something I definitely don't want to discuss with her.

Being upset about men isn't Cilla's style. She's more a buck-up-and-move-on type of girl.

"Aren't we just jet setters? Well, next trip then. Or I could come up to Vancouver to see you. Is it a nice city? Any good action going on up there?"

I think about what I know of the city of Vancouver. Not much. When I'm not on the set, I'm in my hotel room. Other than a few dinners out with my co-star Gavin, I haven't exactly been painting the town red.

"It's very nice there. Very hip. You might like it."

"That sounds like a pretty tepid endorsement, Kristina. Haven't you checked out the scene up there yet? You've been in the damn city for weeks."

Typical Cilla. Nothing, not even work, gets in the way of a good time for her.

"I've been a little busy. You know. With work."

I don't try to mask the sarcasm in my voice. Not that it would matter. Tone of voice isn't something she pays much attention to anyway.

"Work schmerk. You're in a major North American city, Kristina, and you're single. You should be getting out and enjoying life while you're there."

Her reminder that I'm not with Ian anymore makes my chest hurt for a moment. Taking a deep breath in, I lie, "Cilla, I'm just getting to my apartment now. Let me call you back, okay?"

"Sure! Talk to you later, hon!"

As I end the call and stuff my phone back into my purse, I look up to see the cabbie looking back at me in the rearview mirror. "We're a good five blocks from your place, miss."

I can't help but laugh. My cabbie is both weatherman and paternal figure condemning my lying to Cilla. "I know. I guess I just wanted to get off the phone."

We don't say anything more as he takes me to my place, but as I'm about to pay him the fare, he spies Ian's book in the crook of my elbow. Pointing to it, he says excitedly, "I love his books! I didn't know a thing about ancient Rome, but once I began to read him, I actually went to the library for the first time in like twenty years and got myself some books on that time period. Great stuff!"

I look down and see Ian's picture on the back cover, his face so serious as he looks at the camera. He's not like that, though. Not with me. That man is flat and somber. Ian isn't that man at all.

The urge to explain just how wonderful he is—how full of passion for his writing and for me he truly is—bubbles up inside me as the cabbie explains his favorite parts of Caligula's Dream, but I stop myself.

"He writes great books," I say, once again sounding tepid in my praise for something else. When did I become so bland?

"Have a good night."

Nodding, I grab my bag and head up the stairs to my building's front door, stopping for a moment as I unlock it to look around at the little patch of grass and trees across the street. I strain my eyes to scan the area for any sign of him. I'd so hoped beyond hope that he'd be waiting for me.

Waiting to see me.

But there's nothing but rain soaked, leafless

trees and soon-to-be dead grass there.

I BARELY SET my bag down inside my apartment and I can't stand being there. Everything reminds me of how much I miss him, so I quickly leave, unsure of where I should go but desperate to find somewhere in this city that doesn't make me think of him.

The newsstand a block away is closing up as I approach it, but the man knows me from back before I ever made any hit movies, so he waves to me. He's holding something in his hand, and as I walk closer to him I see it's a magazine.

I don't remember Joanne mentioning any magazine covers coming out this month.

"Kristina Richards! How is my favorite famous movie star?"

Mr. Jacobs is a man in his sixties, I guess, with perfectly silver hair. He likes to tell stories of when his hair was black and the women fell at his feet back when he was young and before he married his wife. She's been dead for as long as I've known him, but he speaks about her like she's still at home waiting for him to return every night from his stand in my neighborhood.

"I'm fine. How are you, Mr. Jacobs?"

A huge grin spreads across his face as he holds up the magazine. On the cover is a picture of me looking pretty good considering I think it may have been taken after a long day of shooting. Above my head in bold capital letters are the words ACTRESS KRISTINA RICHARDS IN TORRID LOVE AFFAIR.

Instantly, I'm sick to my stomach as the thought of Ian seeing this races through my mind. Mr. Jacobs asks me who the lucky guy is, so I try to explain The Enquirer has it all wrong. There's no torrid anything in my life and no lucky guy. He arches his brow and gives me a skeptical look, saying, "You just don't want to tell an old man. I see."

Shaking my head, I say, "No, it's not that at all. How long has this been out?"

"About two days."

Now I'm sure Ian's seen it. I know he has. And I can only imagine how much it hurt when he did.

I have to go to him. I hurry off from the newsstand to his building, and as always, his doorman is happy to let me in. Worried how he may have reacted to seeing the headline, I ask, "Have you seen Mr. Anwell this evening?"

His usual jovial look fades a bit as he says, "He went up a few hours ago, miss."

I want to ask more about how he looked and how he seemed, but the doorman won't tell me.

As I ride up in the elevator alone, my heart races at the thought of what I'll say when I finally see him. He's never texted or called after telling me goodbye, so would I find him with a new woman like last time trying to forget me again?

Barely able to keep myself from crying at the thought of finding him with someone else, I walk down his hallway to his door. Taking a deep breath, I knock and pray to God he'll answer and not have someone with him.

I knock three times, but nothing. Pressing my cheek to his door, I listen for any sounds inside, my heart slamming against my chest as the fear that he isn't alone settles into my mind. I hear nothing, though, so I knock again and say, "Ian, are you in there? Please open the door. It's Kristina."

What I get in response is silence. I put my mouth right up to the door and hope if he's inside he's listening. "Ian, I'm here. Please let me in."

Again, silence, but then I hear the door being unlocked. It doesn't open, but I turn the doorknob and see he's at least letting me in. The lights are out and the place is dark except for the light of the TV on the far wall. This doesn't feel like his apartment at all. It's like a pall hangs over the place.

Softly, I ask, "Ian, where are you?"

He says nothing, but as I scan the room for him, I see something on the floor near the couch. Making my way in the dim light, I'm finally able to see now that my eyes have adjusted to the light. It's him.

Sprawled out with a bottle next to him, he looks so different than I've ever seen him. His shirt is half unbuttoned and the shirt sleeves are rolled up past his elbows. In the dim light, I see him staring up at me with a hollow look in his eyes.

I crouch down in front of him and look closer. I've never seen him like this. He looks lost. Reaching out, I caress his cheek with my palm and feel the softness of his skin and the roughness of his beard just coming in.

"Oh, Ian…"

He doesn't move, but I feel his head press against my hand. Then he speaks, and I know he's seen the cover. "Why are you here? Don't you have some torrid love affair to attend to?"

Shaking my head, I try to put a happy face on while my heart is breaking to see him like this. "I missed you."

His words seem to get stuck when he tries to speak, but finally he says in a low voice full of pain, "Five weeks is all it took to forget me, I guess."

I can't stop the tears from welling in my eyes. He's done this to himself because I didn't go with him. No amount of explaining about my job or how important this role is to me will make up for lying and then letting him go. Even now, I realize for as much as this role means to my career, he means more to me than anything.

"Oh, Ian, that's not true." I hang my head and whisper, "I missed you so much. Please don't think I didn't."

In a strangled tone, he asks the question I don't want to answer. "Then why didn't you come to Rome?"

I fall to the floor in a crumbled heap. Unable to hold the tears back, I give him the only answer I can. "I never meant to hurt you. I swear I didn't."

"Well, you did."

He sounds so lonely and sad. I can't stand to hear him like this. I want to make things better, but it's like I can't reach him, even though he's sitting right next to me. It's like there's an invisible barrier between us.

I wrap my arms around his shoulders and pull him into me. He doesn't resist, but he doesn't hug me back either. In his ear, I plead, "Ian, don't shut me out. I'm here. Let me in."

"It's too late."

Leaning back away from him, I shake my head in disbelief. "No, it's not! Put your arms around me. I know you still care. If you don't still love me, then say the words. I won't believe it unless you say the words."

Ian says nothing, but I see something in his expression that tells me it isn't too late for us. I lift his hands to my mouth and kiss them, hoping for any real sign the man I love is still inside him.

"Kristina, you need to leave. I don't want you to see me like this."

Leaning my cheek against his palm, I'm confused by his words. "What do you mean like this? Like what?"

He yanks his hands away from me and shakes his head violently. "Go away. Go back to your new boyfriend and be happy."

"There is no new boyfriend, Ian," I say as I try to pull him back toward me. I need to touch him, but he won't let me now. "I swear there's no one but you. Why won't you believe me?"

"Because you fucking let me go to Rome."

"Well, I'm not going anywhere now, so you're stuck with me."

I can't stand the distance between us even as I sit next to him. Climbing onto his lap, I fight against him pushing me away until he stops and stares up at me with so much hurt in his eyes that

I almost need to turn away.

"You don't want me, Kristina. Not like this."

His head droops until his forehead presses against my shoulder. With a deep sigh, he finally wraps his arms around me and I feel his overwhelming sadness as he pulls me to him.

"Why wouldn't I want you, Ian? I love you. I wanted to go to Rome. I should have. I know that now. I'm sorry I lied. Please don't tell me to leave."

Ian lifts his head, and I see the misery in his eyes. I cradle his face and kiss him, letting all the weeks of missing him come out finally. When he kisses me back, I know how much we've both suffered. His kiss is filled with desperation as much as mine is, and for the first time since that night I met him at that bar, I feel like he truly needs me like I need him.

Closing his eyes, he leans his head back against the wall. "I don't want you to see me like this. You don't want this Ian."

"I want you. It doesn't matter who you are."

"No, you don't. I couldn't stand the pain and missing you, so I went back to it. To heroin. I just wanted to be able to forget."

His words come out practically as sobs that break my heart to hear. He's doing heroin again, and everything I said to him that night he told me about his addiction rings in my ears. But now as I sit here watching him in so much pain, I can't imagine leaving him.

I press my forehead to his. "I won't leave you. I promise."

"Why would you stay when you told me if I ever went back to using again you'd leave me?" he asks quietly.

"Because I love you."

"You won't love me like this, Kristina. You won't."

CHAPTER THREE

Ian

FOR THREE DAYS, Kristina's been here with me, but even that can't make me stop needing the shit I stick up my nose. I don't know why she stays. She shouldn't. She should stick by what she said to me that night I told her what I really am.

The problem is that last night I ran out, which leads to an entirely different problem. The heroin is bad enough. Withdrawal is so much fucking worse.

I lied to her and told her I'm done with the junk. The look of pure happiness she had when I said it made me wish more than anything else in this world that I could give it up.

But I can't. Not yet. Not now.

So this morning, I had my editor send one of his lackeys over with what looks like work but is really just a bag of poison. He's happy to hear I'm off the wagon again, so to speak, since misery always loves company.

And for a little while I'm okay, but like always, it's never enough. By the time Kristina realizes what I am, it will be too late. She'll already hate me so much she won't ever want to see me again. I know all this and still here I am hiding out in the bathroom snorting heroin while she takes a shower in the bathroom down the hall.

I sit back on the tile floor to wait for that feeling to come over me. It doesn't take a half hour like it used to. Maybe that's because I've been clean for nearly a year, but this time it hits me almost immediately. Or maybe I've lost track of time.

I don't know. All I know is that when it hits me and that feeling of euphoria comes over me, I can't think of anything but how much I love feeling like this. No pain. No worries. Nothing but pure bliss.

Only being with Kristina comes close to this, but now that I've got heroin again, even she can't equal this feeling of happiness and contentment. I wish I could feel bad about that, but in this state, no way.

When I'm like this, nothing can bother me.

"Ian, I'm out of the shower. Are you in there?"

I clean up as quickly as possible and stuff the

baggie into my back pocket as I open the bathroom door to see Kristina standing there looking so fresh and sweet. God, I love her.

"Have a good one?" I ask, hoping she doesn't recognize how fucked up I am at the moment.

She giggles. "A shower? I guess. You could have come in if you needed to go to the bathroom. I don't want to monopolize it."

Shaking my head, I smile. "That's what I have two for."

We stand there in silence for a moment as she seems to study me. She's not stupid. After she found me sitting on the floor high, she naturally suspects that even though I say I'm not doing it anymore, I likely am. What she probably can't figure out is how I got it.

Good people like her don't suspect how manipulative and devious people like I can be when we want it.

"What are you planning to do today?"

I pull her to me and nuzzle her neck, knowing that it's a fifty-fifty shot if I can even fuck when I'm this high. I want to, though. I want to be buried in her wet cunt or have her down on her knees sucking my cock right there in the doorway.

"Don't know, but I have some ideas about what I want to do now."

We haven't made love since she came here

three days ago, so my newfound desire for her pleases her more than I imagined. Running her hands down the front of my pants, she unzips them and takes my semi-hard cock in her palm, stroking it from base to tip. I might not be able to get a hard on like this, but the touch of her hand on my skin feels fucking incredible, like every sensation is twenty times more pleasurable than ever before.

Kristina looks down at my hardening cock and licks her lips. "Follow me."

Taking my hand, she leads me to the bedroom, and as I watch mesmerized by how much I love her, she slips out of her clothes and beckons me to her. By the time I reach the bed, I'm out of my own clothes and my cock is more than willing, but I can't be sure if I have to face her while we make love that she won't realize I'm high.

So even though I know it may still upset her, I roll her over on her stomach to take her from behind. She doesn't say a thing and angles her ass high in the air so her pussy is right there for me.

I stuff my hand in her hair and tug her up off the bed as the first inches of my cock are swallowed by her willing cunt. She's hot and wet and all mine.

In her ear, I groan, "God, I fucking need you,

Kristina." I mean more than just to fuck her, but at that moment, she thinks it's just sex talk and moans as the base of my cock pushes up against her body, fully nested inside her.

She's as eager to please me as ever, so once I establish a rhythm in and out of her, she begins her own, meeting my thrusts as she pushes back against me. I love this about Kristina. Whatever we are when my cock is buried inside her isn't just me fucking her but the two of us together moving toward that sweet moment of oblivion when her cunt contracts around me and I flood her with cum.

As I think about all of this, she moans, "Ian, I want it faster. And harder."

Gripping her sides, I ram my hips forward and fill her fast and hard, just as she asked. She gasps but after a moment repeats for me to go faster and harder, pushing back against me as I remain inside her.

As much as I can in my state, I fuck her exactly how she wants it. Her hands grasp at the sheets and she moans over and over as I inch her closer to her release. I feel her body begin to surrender to my invasion, the walls of her cunt gently squeezing around my cock as she orgasms harder than I've ever felt her come before.

"Ian, don't stop! Please don't stop!"

I don't and she continues to shake from coming until I finally pull out, still hard since I haven't come yet. Heroin may make the sensations of sex one hundred percent better, but coming isn't one of those parts that are improved.

Kristina collapses on the bed and rolls over to look up at me. Her expression tells me I satisfied her, but when her gaze falls on my still hard cock, she frowns. "You didn't come. Why?"

I can't tell her the truth, so a little white lie has to serve. "I wanted you to suck me off. You know I like that."

Her frown disappears, replaced by a sexy, devilish grin. "I do. You like to see me taste myself on you, don't you?"

I nod and pull her up toward me, loving the idea of her mouth around my shaft. I still might not get off, but the feeling of her soft lips and tongue riding up and down my cock will still be incredible.

She kisses me so full of love that for a fleeting moment I hate that I'm lying to her as she lowers herself to take my cock inside her mouth. Kneeling in front of me, she looks up and runs her tongue over her lower lip, like she's dying to taste something she loves. Pulling her hair off her face, I close my fist around it while I gently caress her gorgeous mouth that in the next moment I'll fill with my cock.

Any regret for what I've done vanishes the second she gently sucks the head and moans against my skin, sending the most exquisite sensations up and down my shaft. I pull her down hard on me until she's taken every inch and I'm bumping up against the back of her throat. She never closes her eyes as I fuck her mouth just like I fucked her pussy.

I want to come. I want to fill her mouth until cum oozes out the sides and drips down her chin like beautiful lines of white love she gives me. My brain wants to, but my body has other ideas because of the heroin.

Kristina sucks my cock like every stroke down my shaft brings her happiness. Her blue eyes stare up at me waiting for the moment when I look like my release is just upon me, but no matter how long she tries, my body isn't letting it happen.

I massage her jaw, knowing she's hurting, but I don't stop her. I'm selfish and a fucked up prick for not letting her just sit back and have her orgasm without me having one, but I don't push her away. Instead I watch in wonder as her head bobs up and down into my crotch, and with each pass I know it's hopeless.

The junk has taken away another good thing.

Finally, she looks up at me with hurt in her

eyes like she's done something wrong or she's deficient and that's why I haven't come. I shake my head and ease out of her mouth as that twinge of regret finds its way back into my mind.

"I thought you liked how I do that," she says in a sweet voice that makes my heart feel like someone's run it through.

"I do. I just can't now," I answer in the kindest voice I can give.

"Oh. Why?"

I look away, afraid she can see the truth written all over my face. I've never felt so bad when I was high. Was that stuff my editor sent over shit?

"Ian, look at me. What's going on? Is there someone else you haven't told me about?"

Jesus, the pain in her voice is killing me. I can't do this. "Kristina, it's nothing."

The silence that follows makes the room feel like she and I are miles apart and she's receding more and more every second. I can't look at her and see the hurt in her eyes, so I just keep my head hung and wait for her to say something.

Anything but that she needs the truth.

But she doesn't need it. She already knows. "You didn't stop, did you?"

Again, silence, but this time it's me who can't bring myself to say the words. Instead, I just shake my head.

A sound like a gasp is all I hear, and then the bed moves as she stands up. I turn to see her getting dressed.

"Kristina," I begin, but stop, knowing she doesn't deserve some watered down excuse for why I'm like this.

"I should have done what I said I would when you told me what you were. I couldn't, though, so I stayed and believed you. What a fool I am! I've seen this so many times and still I thought you'd give it up for me."

"Don't," is all I can get out. I don't want her blaming herself. She isn't the fucked up one.

"Don't what? Don't feel like an idiot that I believed you and went against everything I knew I should do?"

I sit back against the headboard and close my eyes. I don't want her to blame herself. I just don't know what to say. It's sad, really. A fucking author who can't find the words he needs to say to say to the woman he loves.

"I know you said you'd leave, but don't. Stay. Show me you love me enough to stay."

The sound of her pants rustling as she pulls them on makes me open my eyes, and suddenly, I see her lunging toward me on the bed. Before I can lift my arms, she's on top of me swinging her arms wildly. Her delicate fists hit my face as she sobs words I can't understand.

I deserve whatever she does to me, so I don't try to grab her wrists to stop her. Maybe if she hits me hard enough or I have to watch her cry for long enough I'll finally get it through my head that I shouldn't be a slave to this shit I crave even now.

"Why, Ian? Why would you do this? Am I so unimportant to you that you'd pick drugs over me?"

Her beautiful mouth—the mouth that made me want her from the moment I first laid eyes on her on my television screen—twists into a terrible frown as the tears roll down her cheeks from those cornflower blue eyes I love so much. Her face looks ravaged by sadness.

Sadness I caused her.

"I don't want to do this, Kristina. Believe me. I want to stop."

At the moment I say that, I mean every word. I do. I just can't see how I'll stop, though. It's been only a few weeks, and all the progress I made over the past nine months is all but lost.

"I can't stay here with you. I can't watch you throw your life away, Ian."

She moves to leave, but I can't let her. I can't lose her.

Grabbing her arm as she crawls off the bed, I stare up into those gorgeous eyes so full of pain and worry I can't change her mind. Like when she was sitting there on the floor with me the night she came back, it feels like we're miles apart.

I'm losing her.

"Please don't leave. I'll stop. I swear I will. Tell me what I have to do and I'll do it. Just don't leave."

She shakes her head and begins to cry again. "I can't tell you what to do. That you don't know if you do this you'll lose me tells me all I need. I have to go."

Yanking her hand from my hold, she runs out of the room as I scramble to my feet. I reach her just as she hits the front door, and knowing this might be my last chance to ever convince her I love her, I wrap my arms around her and hold her tight.

"Let me go! I can't do this, Ian! I can't!"

She writhes in my hold and I barely hang on, but finally she stops and collapses against my chest, sobbing, "I can't do this with you. I love you too much to see you ruin us like this."

"Stay with me, Kristina. I'm begging you. Stay even though I'm fucked up. Stay even though I made the biggest mistake and you think you can't forgive me. Just stay."

For the longest moment, she says nothing and all I can think is I've lost her. I laid it all on the line and still she won't stay.

She begins to push against my hold, but instead of leaving she turns around to face me. Her cheeks are tear stained, her eyes rimmed with red, but I see love in them still.

"Why can't I leave you? Why after all these weeks without you does the thought of losing you now make me feel like I'm losing part of myself?"

I cradle her beautiful, sad face and nod because I know exactly what she feels. The mere thought of my life without her in it is too much to bear. Leaning forward, I kiss her with all the desperation inside me and when I finally pull away, I wipe her tears and say, "Because you love me as much as I love you."

"We're a mess, Ian. This love is crazy and hurts so much that I don't think I can go on."

"Stay even though everything you know about me is bad."

Closing her eyes, she presses her forehead to mine. "You aren't bad, Ian. I don't know why you're like this, but you're not bad."

"I'll stop. Don't leave me. I can do this. I can quit it."

"Oh, Ian, what if we can't get through this? What if this is just who you are?"

Pulling her to me, I kiss the top of her head. "I can't believe that. I love you, Kristina. Since the moment I met you, I've been crazy about you."

She hugs me and whispers, "I don't know what to do. I love you so much, but this scares me. You won't pick me when it comes down to it."

"I will. I'm picking you right now. Stay with me no matter what I become, and I promise when this is all over we'll have a new start."

She kisses me with such sadness I'm sure the next word out of her mouth will be goodbye. But then she smiles sweetly and I believe I can give up the junk for her.

CHAPTER FOUR

Kristina

NEVER BEFORE IN my life have I been so certain I was making the wrong choice, and still I don't leave. I look into those nearly jet black eyes staring at me so desperately as Ian waits to hear he hasn't lost me and I can't.

I can't leave him. Whatever this is between us—love, lust, or obsession—I need it. I need him. For the past five weeks I've walked around feeling like part of me had been torn out and what was left when I looked down at my phone and saw him tell me goodbye was an emptiness inside that ached day and night.

But he won't choose me over the drugs. I knew that when I told him I would leave, and I know that now as he pleads for me to stay.

And still I can't say goodbye.

I push his unruly black hair off his forehead and sigh. "I've never been so sure of anything in my life as I am right now that you're going to break my heart."

"Give me the chance to prove you wrong."

Looking down, I can't help but smile. He's naked at his front door begging me to stay. But then I remember he snuck that terrible junk in and it's still somewhere in his apartment. Angrily, I say, "You need to get rid of any you have left, or I'm gone. Period."

He nods, but I can see he won't be able to throw it out. "I don't want this job, Ian, but if I'm going to stay, I'm staying on my terms. That leaves or I leave."

His hand slides down my arm, and he weaves his fingers in mine as he leads me back to the bedroom. Pointing at his pants, he says quietly, "Back pocket. And there's probably a tiny bit left on the edge of the tub in the bathroom."

A surge of anger races through me as I remember standing in the doorway to that bathroom after my shower feeling all clean and fresh and ready to spend the day with him and all the while he was high already. I reach down and find a plastic baggie with white powder in the back pocket of his pants.

"This is it?"

"Yeah," he says in a strained voice as he stares at it in my hand.

"Fine."

Turning on my heels, I walk to the bathroom that until now had held the memory of that incredibly sexy lovemaking session we'd had that one night. From this point on, now that will be joined by the memory of me scrubbing the edge of a fucking bathtub so he can't find any more of his drugs on it.

I flush the powder down the toilet and clean the tub from top to bottom like I've never cleaned before in my life. I'm like a woman on a mission as I scrub and scrub that white marble tub until my right bicep feels like it's going to blow out of my arm. With each push of the sponge, my hair swings in my eyes, and for a moment I remember the bathroom cleaning scene in the movie Mommy Dearest as Faye Dunaway scours that tile floor while her poor little daughter watches on in horror.

The sound of Ian's footsteps on the tile as he enters the bathroom takes me out of my daydreaming, and as I wash away the last of the cleanser from the edge of the tub, I can't help but say, "Some glamourous life of a movie star, huh?"

"I'm sorry, Kristina."

I think he's genuine when he says that. I do. I just don't know if it matters much. I dry my hands on a towel and see my fingertips are all pruney like they used to get when I was a little girl and spent too much time in the bath at night.

Ian looks lost, like he doesn't know what to do with himself. Is he unsure what to do because of how angry I seem or because he's craving more of the heroin I just flushed down the toilet? As if he's reading my mind, he says as he takes my hand to kiss the back of it, "I don't know what to do when you're like this."

"Like what, Ian? Hurt? Angry? Worried that the minute I turn my back on you that you're going to have some guy come to the front door pretending to deliver something from that fuck of an editor?"

Letting my emotions out should make me feel better, but the sad look in his eyes just makes me feel terrible for being so angry at him. Hanging my head, I admit, "I'm no good at this. That's why I told you I'd leave if you went back to doing drugs. I'm not kind enough or sympathetic enough to be what you need now."

"You're exactly what I need now. I don't need someone to believe my lies when I say I don't want heroin more than anything else in the world at this moment. I don't need someone who's worried about hurting my feelings. I need you to kick my ass and make this real for me because if you don't, I won't be able to do this."

I sit on the damp edge of the tub and look up

at him. "Do you really want to keep doing that more than anything?"

His expression twists into a grimace, like what I said hurt him, and he nods. "Yeah. That's how it is with me and heroin. Nearly a year without it, and now all I want is more."

"More than me," I say sadly, hating the truth.

Ian takes my hands in his and squeezes them. "No, not more than you. It's not the same. I love you. I need you. That shit fucks me up and takes control of me. You make me happier than I've ever been before in my life."

"You said you were addicted to me. Why can't you want me more than you want this?"

I sound childish and naïve, but that's how I feel. The fact that he could feel more for some white powder in a plastic bag than he feels for me is tearing me up inside. No matter how I try, I can't understand how that could be.

He gently pushes my hair out of my eyes and bends down to kiss my forehead as he whispers, "I hate that my weakness makes you doubt yourself. Don't do that."

I hang my head, and he pulls me to him to hold me. With my cheek pressed against his side, I tell him the truth. "I love you, Ian, but this hurts so much. Why did you have to go back to that awful stuff?"

As he gently strokes my hair, he says, "I'm an addict, and I turned to the one thing that I knew could take the pain away. I'm sorry, baby. I'm so sorry I'm like this."

Looking up at him, I see he's hurting still. "Why didn't you just call me? I would have taken the pain away."

"You were the reason I was in pain. I missed you so much while I was in Italy and couldn't deal with it, and then when I saw that magazine that said you were in a torrid love affair, I just wanted to forget. I just wanted to close my eyes and not hurt anymore."

Tears fill my eyes as I say, "There's no one else, Ian. Not since the day we met. You're all I think about, even during those five weeks after you said goodbye."

"I'm sorry, Kristina. I was just so torn up by how easy it seemed for you to let me go…"

Before he can finish what he's saying, I stand and shake my head at how wrong he is. "It wasn't easy to let you go to Italy without me. I wanted to go, but Joanne found out what I was planning and I couldn't. I know I should have, but I wanted this part so badly." I stop and take a deep breath. "Oh, what does it matter now? If I didn't stay, if you didn't go. It doesn't matter anymore."

He cradles my face in his hands and stares

down into my eyes with so much regret that my chest tightens at seeing him like this. "I did this to us. You didn't do anything wrong. I wanted to think you did because you chose something over me, but you're here with me and I don't want to think about the mistakes we've made or the time we've lost."

"But what happens now?" I ask, almost afraid to know the answer.

"I'm going to have to kick this, but it's going to be hard for you. Everything about me is going to be nothing but bad, but I swear if you stay, I'll stop."

"Hard for me? Why?"

"I'm not going to look or act like myself as this poison leaves me. I'm going to want it more than anything, and when I can't have it, I'm going to get ugly. I just want to tell you now that I love you and when I say those things that hurt you, it's not me talking. It's the addiction."

I don't know if I can handle what he's going to be like, but I don't have a choice. I love him.

WITHIN TWO DAYS, I see firsthand the ugly Ian had promised. Already in withdrawal, he looks like a twisted, horrific version of himself. I roll over as I wake in the morning and see him staring not at me but at the wall. His eyes look wild, and his skin glistens with a layer of sweat, even though it's winter outside and no warmer than seventy degrees in his apartment.

Reaching out, I go to push his hair off his damp forehead and feel his skin. It's cold even as he lies there sweating on top of the blankets. My touch makes him cringe, as if anything on his skin hurts.

"Ian, tell me what I'm supposed to do. You look so lost and in so much pain."

"Just don't go. This isn't too bad yet. When it gets bad, please don't leave me here alone or I'll find some way to get more so I don't have to go through this."

"How long will this last?"

Frowning, he shakes his head. "I don't know. A few days, maybe. I only used for a short time this time, so maybe it won't be so long. I've never stopped without going to rehab, though, so I don't know."

He curls up next to me, and I want to take him in my arms and never let him go he looks so broken and hurt. Over and over, he begs me not to leave. "I'm not going anywhere, Ian. I promise."

I gently pull him to me and he whispers so quietly against my shoulder that I can barely hear him, "I can't do this alone. Please don't leave me."

There in his bed as I lie with him in my arms, I promise him something I've never been able to promise anyone else before. "No matter what, I'll be strong for you. I won't leave you."

For hours, I stay beside him as he shakes almost uncontrollably one minute and then seems so tired he can't even keep his eyes open the next. I've never seen him so vulnerable and weak, and all I want to do is keep my promise to him to be the strength he needs.

But that part of me that's never been strong makes me doubt I can do this.

As it begins to get dark outside, Ian slowly opens his eyes and I see the fear and pain he's going through in them. "Every inch of my body hurts. I can't take this pain, baby."

"It won't be for long," I whisper as he curls up next to me, shivering even as his skin is hot against mine. "I promise it won't be for much longer."

That promise is one I can't keep because I have no idea how long he'll be like this. Even worse, my phone has been vibrating every hour on the hour, and I know it's my agent wanting to know why I'm not back in Vancouver on the set. I've avoided her all day, but I can't ignore her forever.

"I'm so thirsty. Can you get me a glass of water?"

"Okay. I'll be right back," I say as I cover him with the sheet and blanket. As I leave, I grab my phone to call Jennie and try to figure out how I'm going to explain to her that I can't go back yet.

That Ian needs me more than I need any role, and I won't leave him now.

Alone in his living room, I dial her number and prepare myself for the lecture I'm bound to get. Looking out the floor to ceiling windows that show me the city below, I hear the panic in her voice as she answers.

"Kristina, where are you? I've been calling you all day. You were supposed to be back on set this afternoon, but they say you aren't there. What's going on?"

"Jennie, I can't explain everything, but I'm not going to be able to leave New York just yet. I need you to make some excuse so I can stay here and still be able to go back to the set when I can."

"What? You have to get back there, Kristina. An entire production can't shut down for just nothing."

I look around to make sure Ian is still in the bedroom and whisper, "This isn't nothing. Someone I care about a great deal needs my help, and I can't abandon them now. Please, I'm begging you. I need you to help me. Just tell them I need a little more time. Make something up."

"Kristina, is this the torrid love affair guy from the magazine article?"

I think about Ian going through withdrawal in his bedroom and try to remember when we were torrid lovers. Smiling, I say to her, "Yes. I can't leave him now. He needs me, and I can't let him down. So tell them I'll be back in a few days more."

Jennie lets out a big sigh. "I hope you know what you're doing, honey. Okay, I'll tell them you're sick. Everyone gets sick, right? I'll say it's the flu and you're laid up sick as a dog."

"Tell them whatever you have to. I promise I'll be back in Vancouver within the week, okay?"

"Okay. Take care of yourself, Kristina. I don't want to see you get hurt."

"Thank you, Jennie. Don't worry about me. I'll be okay."

I press END and let out a sigh of relief. At least I have a few more days to be there for Ian before I'd have to return to the set. I have no idea what will happen in that time, but I can't leave him in the state he's in now.

"Kristina! Where are you?" he says in a voice more like a groan as I walk back to the bedroom with his glass of water.

I stop in the doorway at the sight of him sitting on the edge of the bed. His black hair hangs in damp clumps over his face, and his shoulders hunch over as if he's holding the weight of the world on them. His breath is coming in shallow pants, and I worry that something has happened in the few minutes I was away.

Hurrying to his side, I sit down next to him and practically feel the waves of misery coming off him. "What happened? Why aren't you in bed?"

"I was thirsty, and I didn't know where you went or if you were still here at all. I wanted to get a drink, but when I stood up, my legs gave out."

He turns to look at me and spies the glass of water in my hand. Reaching out for it, he shakes so badly I'm sure he'll drop it if I let go, so I hold it to his lips and tilt it back slightly so only a tiny bit flows into his mouth. I pull the glass away, but he grabs my hand and gently squeezes it.

"I'm so thirsty. A little more."

"It's okay. Just let me hold it. You're too weak from being in bed for so long."

Ian takes another small gulp of water, and as I take the glass away, he looks over at me and gives me a gentle smile. "I'm weak because my body is craving that poison, Kristina. You don't need to sugarcoat it."

I nod to show I understand, but I truly don't.

I want to help him through this, but I'm so ignorant of everything he's feeling.

"I didn't mean to…" I let my thought trail off because I don't know what to apologize for. Instead, I press a smile onto my lips and try to sound as happy as possible, hoping that helps in some small way. "Let's get you back into bed."

He doesn't fight my suggestion, although I'm not even sure being in bed is helpful in his condition. I help him back under the covers and crawl under them myself, suddenly more tired than I've been in years.

"Are you feeling better now?" I ask as he rests his head on the pillow next to me.

Knitting his brows, he frowns at my question. "No. Worse, actually."

I press the back of my hand to his forehead and feel his skin dry and cool for the first time in hours. "You don't feel hot anymore."

As I pull my hand away, he holds it and presses his dry lips to my fingertips in a kiss. Then he looks at me with those dark eyes that still seem so lost and says, "I don't have the twenty-four hour flu, baby."

"I know. I mean, I don't know what to say here. I don't know what you're going through, so I don't know how to act," I explain, barely holding back the emotional tidal wave inside me.

"You don't have to act any way other than who you naturally are. I love you for not leaving, even though you never signed on for this with me."

My conversation with Jennie weighs on my mind as I watch him struggle to relax. He tosses and turns in what looks like agony over and over, and then just when I think it can't get any worse, he stumbles from the bed to the bathroom and makes a retching noise so terrible I jump up and run to see if he's still alive.

What I see is so much worse than everything I've watched him go through already. On his knees and holding onto the bowl of the toilet, he vomits for nearly ten minutes straight, his shoulders and back violently undulating with each heave. I stand behind him rubbing his skin and ready to help, but I can't do this.

I'm not enough. He needs more than I can give him.

Ian finally sits down on the floor and leans back against the vanity. Clearly exhausted, he looks like a shell of the man I met a few months ago as he wipes his mouth clean. I can't watch him like this anymore. It's breaking my heart.

I sit on the floor next to him and take his hand, knowing what I have to say next isn't what he wants to hear. But it's what he needs to hear.

So with my emotions ready to boil over, I say quietly, "I'm not what you need, Ian. You're not going to get better like this, are you?"

Hanging his head, he slowly shakes his head. "No."

"We need to get you better, baby, so tell me what you need me to do so that can happen. Wherever you need to go, I'll get you there."

His voice raspy, he says, "Meadowbrook. My agent knows all the details. Get me my phone, please?"

I get him the cell phone and watch as he calls her to let her know he's messed up again. The pain and regret in his voice is almost too much to bear, but from what I can hear of his side of the conversation, she's understanding.

Ian hands me the phone and buries his face in his hands. My eyes fill with tears as before me what's left of him falls apart. Taking him in my arms, I feel the sadness he can't keep in anymore as his body sags against mine.

"I'm sorry, Kristina. I'm so sorry."

"Don't worry. You'll get better, and by the time you get home, I'll be back and we can pick up where we left off before all that Rome stuff and this happened."

I want so much to be able to put all that behind us, even as the fear that we can't sits in the back of my mind terrifying me. He looks up at me and all I want to do is take his pain away.

"I love you. Forgive me."

Holding him to me, I know he loves me as I love him. But is that enough? After everything we've been through, is love enough?

CHAPTER FIVE

Ian

I STEP OUT into the January chill of northern Arizona and shield my eyes from the sun beaming down on the front of Meadowbrook Drug Rehabilitation Center. Six weeks of no drugs or alcohol seems to have made me as sensitive to sunlight as a vampire, and I step back into the building to wait for Sheila, happy to be finally going home.

She's been her usual wonderful self during all of this. Somehow, she's found a way to keep my current stint in rehab off the radar of my publishers and virtually every other person on earth. I don't know how she does it, but without her, I'd be lost.

And Kristina.

Some days, the only way I got through the hours without going clear out of my fucking mind was reading her letters to me. Every week, she sent me two. The first always sounded upbeat and sweet, and the second always sounded like she felt like I did.

Like she didn't know if she could go on being there while I was here.

Just knowing I wasn't alone in this kept me sane when all I wanted to do was unravel and never come back from it. My Kristina. After watching me hit rock bottom, she was the one who'd been brave enough to see I couldn't shake my addiction without more help than she could give me. I couldn't see that, but she could.

I love her for that and everything else she's given me.

I'm ready to return to her and make up for all the bad I've done. Running my hand through my hair, I take a deep breath and love how good I feel. Healthy and good, just like she deserves.

All her letters are stored in the bag I brought with me here, and I open it up to read her last letter she sent just two days ago. Full of love and her worry for me, I cherish it like every other one she sent.

Dear Ian,

As I sit here hundreds of miles away from where you are, I feel like I'm missing a part of me. I know you had to go there, but I can't tell you how lonely I feel. Every day I say my lines and deliver a performance I try to be proud of, but I don't have you to share it with. I wish you were here so every night we could lie in bed and I could tell you all about my day. I so wish I could see the proud look in your eyes.

And then I think of everything you're going through there and feel ashamed that I'm here at all. How could I have ever thought this role was more important than you?

I believe in us, Ian. I know it's been hard, and you still have a little more to go through, but I know when we're finally together again, all the bad we've had to deal with will fade away as long as we remember we love each other.

The next time I see you will be like the first time. Do you remember that night at Jax's? I can't wait for that moment when I get to look into your dark eyes and feel that thrill I felt that first night we met. I'll see you soon, baby. Until then, I love you and can't stop thinking about you.

Love,
Kristina

I fold her letter and slip it back into the envelope as I think back to our first night, smiling at the memory of how much I wanted her even then. Since that first moment when she became more than just a face on the screen, I've loved her.

"Mr. Anwell?"

I look up and see one of the facility's staff members smiling down at me. "Yes?"

"Your ride is here. It's time to go."

Sheila walks through the front doors and comes toward me with her arms open. I think she might even be happier than I am that I'm finally leaving. "Ian, you look wonderful!"

For once, I think the same about her. She's wearing jeans and a grey sweater, a look that's quite casual for her but one that she wears well. When she releases me from her hug, I say, "You look great too, Sheila. Decidedly unprofessional for once, and it looks good on you."

She rolls her eyes and blushes. "On top of getting clean, they gave you even more personality. I approve."

Grabbing my bag, I chuckle. "Well, this place is the best in the country."

"I have so much to tell you. While I was busy hiding all of this from New York, I've been greasing all sorts of wheels for your career. I'll tell you all about it on the plane ride back. For now, we need to go or we're going to be stuck in the desert, and this is definitely not the place for me. Way too dry here."

"I don't want to stay another minute longer than I have to. I've got too much to go back home for," I say as we walk out to the cab.

Sheila winks at me as we climb into the back seat and drive away. "Does this have anything to do with that woman who was at your place the day I came to take you here?"

"Yeah, it does. I didn't just get clean for me but for her too."

"I've never heard you talk about anyone like that, Ian, and I've known you for years. I like hearing you say things like that."

"You never know. All this happiness might make me lose my edge," I joke, hoping to lighten things up a bit.

Sheila shakes her head and puts on a serious look. "No, it's not like that. When you're really happy in life, you can do anything, and that includes writing another fantastic book."

"I had no idea you were such a romantic. I thought you were only a literary agent shark."

"I'm not kidding, Ian. I hope you have some happiness. You deserve it. Maybe being with this woman will help you silence your demons."

Her reference to my drug use does what my kidding couldn't, and suddenly, the mood between us turns more serious than ever before. I owe Sheila everything, and it's time I told her that.

"I can't thank you enough for what you did. Every time, I mean. You've been so much more than just an agent, and I don't tell you that enough."

"You're a great talent, Ian. It's my job to make sure you have what you need to nurture that talent."

"You know that's not all you do, so don't try to be humble. I wouldn't be alive today if you hadn't been there to save me from myself all these times when I got lost in that shit. I owe you everything. I just wanted to say thank you."

She gets all choked up and looks away out her window. A few seconds later when she's composed herself, she turns back to look at me. "Do you know that's the first time you've ever said anything like that to me? Not that I need to hear it, but it's nice."

"I should have said that a long time ago. Thanks for not giving up on me."

"Me give up on my favorite author? Never. But even though I've said this before, I mean it. I hope I never have to do that again."

"Never again. I promise. This time was worse than any other time before. I can't keep being that person anymore."

"You've got a lot to be thankful for, Ian. I

hope you remember that the next time those demons make you think that horrible stuff will make you happy."

"I promise. No more."

Sheila looks genuinely thrilled to hear me swear I won't go back to heroin again, but even more, I'm happy to say the words and truly mean them.

I LEAVE HER in the back of the cab outside my building and see the doorman standing at the front door ready to greet me with a smile. "Mr. Anwell, it's wonderful to see you."

"Thank you, Michael. It's good to be home."

I called Kristina when we landed, but my call went directly to voicemail. The flight got in early, so I'm about an hour ahead of my scheduled time to get home. Once I get settled in, I'll call her again because I'm dying to see her.

Unlocking my apartment door, I smell her perfume as soon as I walk in. It's been weeks and still she's right there with me. I put my bag down and head toward the couch, needing to relax after the flight back. I take a deep breath, loving the scent of her and the memories it brings back, and close my eyes. Soon we'll be back together again.

A noise down the hall makes me sit up, but

before I can move to check it out, I see her walk into my living room like an angel appearing just for me. As she walks toward me, I'm speechless at how happy I am to see her.

Kristina looks down toward her hands as she fidgets with them. "I thought I'd surprise you and be waiting for you when you opened the door, but then you got back early and I didn't want to frighten you."

"It's okay. Come here. I missed you so much. I just want to feel you in my arms."

She steps forward, and I envelop her in a hug that I never want to end as she sobs, "Oh, Ian, you look so wonderful! Are you…better?"

"I am," I say, unable to keep the smile from my face as I look at her. "You're such a sight for sore eyes. I've missed you, Kristina."

Leaning back, she cradles my face and stares into my eyes, as if trying to make up for all the lost time between us. "Every night I thought about you and how much I wished you were lying there next to me. I was so lonely without you."

"No more lonely nights. I promise. I'm done with all of it. I swear."

"I was so worried that you wouldn't be able to forgive me for not being what you needed," she says sadly. "I wanted to be, Ian. I did. I just wasn't enough."

"This was never meant to be on your shoulders, Kristina. It was unfair of me to ask you to help me."

"But I wanted to! I did. I just wanted to be strong for you, but I wasn't enough."

I shake my head and pull her close. "No more about not being enough. You're always just what I need, and you did for me what I couldn't do. You saw what I wouldn't. Without you, I don't know what would have happened, so no more about not being enough."

Quietly, we stand there in each other's arms and together find again what has always been so much a part of us. With each minute that passes, the passion and need we brought out in one another returns, and as I look down into those beautiful blue eyes, I know I'm home.

"Tonight, I'm going to begin making up for all the lost time. I'm going to worship you like you deserve, showing you how much I adore you, Kristina, and when I'm done, I'm going to start all over again so I can be sure you know I love you."

"I love the way you always know the perfect words to say. From the first moment we met, I've loved that. And I love you, Ian, with all my heart. I swear I do."

There in her eyes I see that same look I saw

the night I went with that woman. Fear and insecurity stare back at me. But she doesn't have to worry. There is no one and nothing else I love more, and tonight I'll show her that.

Dipping my head, I nuzzle the tender skin under her left ear and whisper, "I could use a long shower. Let's get this reunion started off fresh and clean."

She smiles and I take her by the hand to lead her to the bathroom where I watched her scrub away the last remnants of my demons. She gently squeezes my hand as we walk into the room, a sign she hasn't forgotten that awful day, but I want her to see that man is no more and the Ian who stands before her is the man she fell in love with.

"It's okay. Trust me?"

Her cornflower blue eyes grow wide for a moment and she nods, giving me a tiny smile I know masks her uncertainty. "I do trust you, Ian. I just…this room only makes me think of that day."

As I slide her dress down her body, I kiss the soft skin of her shoulders and assure her I intend to change her mind about this place. "I promise after tonight this room will only have the sweetest, most exquisite memories for you."

Her dress pools at her feet, leaving her

standing in just black stiletto leather boots and a garter belt. God, she knows how to make me want her!

"I wanted to dress like I did that first night. You like?" she asks with a sparkle in her eyes.

Pulling her into my arms, I slide my hands down her back to cup her ass. "I definitely like. You look sexier than I even remembered."

"I think you're overdressed then." She fumbles with the button on my pants, finally getting it unbuttoned so she can reach in and wrap her hand around my rapidly hardening cock. "We better get you out of these clothes so I'm not the only one ready for a night of hot sex."

"Hot isn't the word for it. Try scorching."

The feel of her palm sliding up my cock is better than anything I can imagine at that moment. It's been so long since anyone but me has touched any part of my body that I worry I might not last long the first time. I take a sharp breath in when she reaches the head, sure a minute more of this sweet torture will be the end of me.

I rip off my shirt and pants, throwing them off to the side, before I lift Kristina so her pussy is the perfect angle for me to thrust my cock in and bury myself in her. She's warm and wet and I enter her with one hard thrust.

"I've waited so fucking long to feel this," I groan as she rolls her hips back and forth, nearly making the top of my head blow off.

Kristina wraps her arms around my neck, and in a voice sexier than I've ever heard from her, whispers in my ear, "Fuck me. Fuck me hard and make me forget everything but your cock."

There isn't anything else in the world I'd rather do than give her just that, so I walk us over to the wall and plant my hands against the cool tile. I kiss her with all the love I have and say, "Hang on and don't let go until I make you come so fucking hard you can't take it anymore."

I feel her fingers thread together behind my neck, and I pull my hips back so only the tip of my cock remains inside her. She stares at me waiting for me to begin fucking her in earnest and smiles as she says, "Fuck me. Please…"

Ramming my cock into her, I do just that and fuck her harder than ever before. I don't last long the first time, but I don't stop. My cum only makes her cunt slicker, and I love the feel of my cock gliding over her wet skin as I bury myself in her. Each thrust elicits a gentle moan from her that only spurs me on, and by the time it's time for her to come, I'm nearly there for my second release.

Kristina bucks against me, her hips and mine

crashing into each other as she rides me to that orgasm I need to give her. Her mouth devours mine with kisses that nearly take my breath away and my legs feel like they're going to give out, but I can't stop until I give her what she wants.

"Ian," she pants softly in my ear, "I'm so close. Give me what I need."

Her cunt begins to gently squeeze my cock and I know she's close. Just one more pump into her and she'll come apart all over me. Rearing back, I thrust once more and bury myself balls deep into her, and that's all it takes.

Every inch of her body tenses, and she drags her nails across my back, clawing as her orgasm rips through her. She's raw and sensual and more beautiful than she's ever been to me in that moment when her body finally surrenders to me again. I continue fucking her to my own release as she whimpers in my ear, "I love you, Ian. More than you know."

I stand there holding her to me, each of us panting after our lovemaking. It's been months since we've truly been with one another, and I don't want this to end. Not the sex but the closeness I've missed between us.

"That was incredible," she says, sweetly smiling at me. "It reminded me of the first time we were together."

"Then we can think of this as our second first time together," I suggest as I place a kiss on the tip of her nose.

"I like that. And I like this room again."

Pressing my forehead to hers, I close my eyes and tell her what I've waited all those weeks to say. "I'm sorry I ever hurt you, Kristina. I was selfish. I know what losing you feels like now, and I never want to feel that pain again. No drug, no anything in this world makes me feel as wonderful as you do."

She smiles, and in that moment, I'm happier than I thought I ever could be.

CHAPTER SIX

Kristina

OPENING MY EYES, I feel Ian's chest beneath my cheek and feel safe. That being with him could bring out a feeling of security after all we'd been through with his drug addiction seems odd, but it's as if our relationship has weathered a trial by fire of sorts and we've come out even stronger on the other side.

I look up and see him still sleeping peacefully, his long, dark lashes resting against his skin, hiding those dark eyes so full of passion all the time. When I arrived here yesterday to surprise him when he returned, I hadn't been sure what he'd be like after all those weeks in rehab. The last I'd seen of him had devastated me—those beautiful eyes of his filled with tears as he accepted his defeat to that awful drug and that he'd have to leave me to try to be the man he wanted to be again.

But it only took a moment for me to see that

the man who'd returned to me was the Ian I'd fallen madly and passionately in love with, and if there had been any doubt, our lovemaking a short time later erased any fears I'd had about us.

Ian stirs and his hand lands gently on the back of my head as I think all of this, and now all I feel is remorse at the doubt I'd harbored. If only I could have been as sure as he was all those weeks he was away…

I never meant for anything to happen. All Vancouver was supposed to be was work, but when he went to rehab and I returned to the set, I couldn't get the sight of him hitting rock bottom out of my mind. It haunted me day and night, and before long, everyone around me could tell something had happened while I was back in New York and not the flu my agent had claimed.

The sadness I felt inside showed in everything I did, and in that weakness I let someone in to make it go away for even a little while. All I'd wanted was someone to talk to, a friend to listen as I talked about how devastated seeing Ian like that had been for me. But when I tried to talk about how I felt, I couldn't because of the promise I'd made him to keep our relationship a secret.

So the sadness remained without my being able to express why I felt so unhappy all the time.

I could act like I was happy on set, but as soon as the cameras stopped rolling, it was too much to bear and someone recognized that.

I never meant for anything to happen. One day Gavin was making jokes between scenes, and I smiled for the first time in days. One smile but it felt so good to be happy again. Then the next day he brought me coffee with a smiley face drawn on the cup and the words "Let's make it a great day!" written down the side. I didn't think anything of it.

And then he asked me if I'd like to grab a bite to eat and one drink led to another and before I knew it, I was naked in his arms back at his hotel room having sex with my co-star. It wasn't meaningful or even very good sex. It was just one sad and vulnerable person looking for comfort where she shouldn't have.

Ian moves his arm to tighten his hold on me and mumbles, "You up?"

Forcing a smile, I look up and see him gazing down at me with that look of love that used to make me feel like the luckiest woman in the world. Now it just makes me feel guilty as hell.

"Yeah. Want me to make some coffee?" I ask as I roll off him, eager to get away and hopefully lessen how bad I feel at this moment.

He grabs my hand before I can get far and

tugs me back onto the bed next to him. "What's the hurry? We have all day, don't we?"

I have nowhere I really need to be. He knows that. Shooting is over, so I don't have to return to Vancouver, thankfully, and I've cleared the next few days to be with him. The problem is that every minute I'm with him I feel guiltier than the last.

"We do, but I thought you'd like to get back to writing. If I remember correctly, you said you wanted to write a sequel to Silk, didn't you?"

Just saying that makes me feel so fucking shitty. Now I'm using something that means so much to both of us as a reason to leave him because I'm wracked with guilt.

Ian gives me a sexy grin and runs his hands down my back to playfully squeeze my ass. "I do want to write that, but I think I need more research."

When he's sweet like this, all I want to do is stay here in his arms and forget the rest of the world exists outside of his bedroom. I want all the bad things we've done to each other to disappear so we can be happy forever right here in this bed.

As we make love, he's tender but powerful, exactly what I fell in love with all those months ago. His mouth excites me like no other man's can, and still only his cock makes me come. Each time he thrusts his body into mine, I love the feelings only he can bring out in me.

Yet still I can't forget what I've done. I live in terror that he's going to find out, and I'll lose the man I love over a couple nights of mediocre sex in a few moments of weakness.

As I STAND at his kitchen counter drinking morning coffee and watching him search through his laptop for what he began writing before he left, all I can think of is getting out of this apartment. I don't want to leave him now, but I worry the guilt is written all over my face. I need to contact Gavin and make sure he doesn't say anything to anyone about what happened between us. Maybe if he doesn't, I'll be able to find a way to live with what I did.

"My agent messaged me that she wants to meet with me ASAP," I lie.

Looking up from his computer, Ian smiles. "I guess I'll have no reason now not to get back to work, huh? Will you be back for dinner? I'm thinking I should make that risotto that you loved again."

Oh, God. How could I have cheated on someone so incredible? What the hell is wrong with me? The man was in rehab after going back to drugs because I broke his heart and my way of dealing with my sadness and loneliness while he was trying to straighten out his life was to sleep with another man?

"Okay. I'll be back for around five. Sound good? You should be able to get a lot written in that time."

Again, I use our book as manipulation. I'm such an awful person. When he leaves me, I won't even have the right to want him back after being such a rotten fucking woman.

Ian turns from his laptop and wraps his arms around my waist. Kissing me sweetly, he cradles my face and says, "I'm calling it Silk and Steel, and I have great news. While I was gone, Silk has continued selling well after hitting the bestseller lists and I've had a few agents contact T. Anderson about the rights."

"You'd leave Sheila after all she's done for you?"

"She doesn't represent this genre. I guess it seems pretty rotten of me not to go with her, but really, she doesn't do romance and erotica."

I look at his gorgeous face and can't help but get lost in those dark eyes of his. "Rotten? I don't think you're rotten. Ever."

He pulls me to him, whispering, "Thank you for forgiving me, Kristina. I know it wasn't easy to be around me while I was fucked up. Thank you for not leaving me."

Oh, Jesus! I'm going to die from the guilt if he keeps talking like this. I have to leave before he sees something's wrong, so I kiss him and force another smile. "Five o'clock, right? I'm looking forward to that risotto."

As he walks me to the front door, he says in a sexy voice, "And that will only be the beginning of our night. Drink lots of coffee today because I plan on keeping you up into the early morning hours."

I roll my eyes and smile even though I feel like a completely horrible person. "You're going to spoil me."

"Good. You deserve it. Now go so I can get to writing our story. I love you."

Even as I tell him I love him, I know it's just a matter of time before he finds out what I've done. God, what am I going to do?

I CALL SIENNA as soon as I hit the sidewalk outside Ian's building and pray she can help me figure out how to fix what I've done before he finds out and I lose the best thing in my life. She'll have some idea what I can do.

"Kristina! Tell me you're in New York!" she says excitedly into the phone.

"I am. Are you?"

"Yes! We have to get together. What are you doing now?"

"I'm calling you to save my life. I need your help, Sienna. I've made a horrible mistake, and I need you to help me fix it."

"You made a horrible mistake? I think you've made like a handful in your life, so I doubt this is that bad. I think that café you and I like is open, so meet me there in twenty and we'll solve your life crisis over some lunch and I can tell you about my new man."

"A new one or the one you were spending all your time in bed with the last time I talked to you?" I ask as I hail a cab.

"A new one! You have to keep up, girl. I'll tell you all about it when I see you. Twenty minutes."

I hang up and climb into the cab to take me to our favorite café and hopefully the solution to the mess I've created. If I can just figure out how to fix this, I know Ian and I can be happy.

SIENNA WAVES TO me as I stand at the hostess desk just inside Surge, a café more known for its decadent milkshakes than anything else. A hangout for us from years ago, its name has changed a few times since then but we still love it.

I walk through the maze of teakwood tables to

join her at a back table and find she's all ready for our chat with coffee and my favorite blueberry muffins. Taking a seat, I notice the chair next to hers is pushed out.

"Did you bring that new guy with you?" I ask, hoping her answer is no.

"No. He's back at my place. Cilla is sitting here, but she had to run to the ladies' room."

"Sienna! I wanted to talk to you. Alone."

"I'm sorry. She grabbed me as I was heading out the door. I guess she's got some tragedy of her own she's dealing with. But it's okay, Kristina. We're all friends, and she knows what's said here stays here."

As Sienna finishes speaking, Cilla sits down in front of me and gives my arm a gentle squeeze. "I hear you're as unhappy as I am, honey. You know what they say. Misery loves company, right?"

"I guess. What's wrong?" I ask, hoping to keep her focused on her own misery.

"My accountant. The fucker has embezzled almost all my money!" she answers with tears in her eyes.

"Oh, I'm sorry, Cilla. What are you going to do?"

"She's back to sleeping with that awful ex-husband of hers is what she's doing," Sienna says with a tone of disgust that matches her expression.

Never a fan of Priscilla's second husband, Rafe, she's always referred to him as "The Creeper" for how close an eye he kept on Cilla when they were together.

"I don't have a choice," Cilla whines. "It's not like I can just meet a man and get him to pay all my bills. Maybe ten years ago, but now as I slog toward thirty? No way."

"Enough about Cilla and The Creeper. Tell us about your tale of woe, Kristina. We might even be able to do something about that. Accountants with sticky fingers will have to be handled by the cops."

Suddenly, this doesn't seem like a good idea anymore. Sienna I can trust, but I'm not sure about Cilla. She has a nasty habit of gossiping too much. But I need Sienna's advice, so if that means Cilla has to hear some things, so be it. As long as I keep Ian's name out of everything, I should be fine.

I take a deep breath and say, "I need advice about a romance problem."

Sienna elbows Cilla nearly off the chair. "See? Now this is something I can help with. Go on, Kristina. What is it?"

"I've been seeing someone and he had to go away for a little bit, and well, I was lonely and I…" I couldn't say the words.

"You cheated on him. Got it. Were you two broken up at the time?" Sienna asks.

Shaking my head, I say quietly, "No. He had to go to rehab."

"You cheated on your boyfriend while he was in rehab, Kristina? That's not like you. You're usually the incredibly supportive girlfriend," Cilla says with a tone of judgment I don't appreciate.

"It's not like you think. Whatever. But I don't want him to find out and have that send him back to using."

Sienna wrinkles her nose. "I don't think you should hold yourself responsible for him falling off the wagon, if he does. I'm just surprised you're with someone who's into drugs at all, though. That's definitely not like you."

"He isn't. Well, he wasn't when we got together. It's just that when I didn't go to Rome with him, he got back into it. So you see, I don't want that to happen again. I don't know what to do."

"This is the Rome guy? I guess he didn't take the bad news well. Wow."

Cilla's gaze bounces back and forth between Sienna and me as she tries to keep up with the story. "Who? What are we talking about? How about some names so I know what's going on here?"

Turning toward her, Sienna explains, "Kristina's been seeing this guy who wanted her to go to Rome with him. She lied to him and said she would, but she couldn't when it came right down to it because she had to go shoot in Vancouver. When she didn't show, he unraveled and got back into drugs."

Cilla nods like she understands, and then Sienna turns back to face me. "What kinds of drugs are we talking about here? Prescription stuff? Oxy? Cause that stuff is a bitch to kick."

"No, not Oxy. Heroin," I say quietly, already hating that the conversation has become fixated on Ian's drug problem.

"You're dating a heroin addict, Kristina? What is going on with you?" Cilla asks, still confused but willing to give her unsolicited opinion on my love life.

"Sienna, I need to know what to do about the other problem. Could we get back to that?"

Unlike Cilla, Sienna can take a hint, so she smiles and says, "Okay, I'm sorry. The whole drug thing isn't really the issue we should be talking about. You had a moment of weakness while he was in rehab and you don't want him to find out, right?"

"Yes. What do I do?"

"I think you have to go to the guy you were

with and tell him it's important to keep this whole thing on the down-low. Who is it? Maybe we have some dirt on him that we can use to keep his mouth shut."

See, this is why I knew Sienna could help. I'd never think of anything like that.

I look around to see if anyone is close enough to our table to hear what I have to say and then lean in toward Sienna. "Gavin Somers. He was the lead in that movie I was filming in Vancouver. It only happened twice, but I don't want this to get out."

"Our lips are sealed, Kristina," Sienna says to assure me. "Right, Cilla?"

Cilla quickly nods. "Of course. Sealed shut."

"So I should tell him I need him to keep this to himself? What if he won't?"

"Then we get something on him and ruin his fucking life. Scorched earth, baby," Sienna says nonchalantly before she takes a sip of coffee.

"I'm not really a fan of the scorched earth policy. I mean, the whole thing with him was a mistake I'd just rather put behind me and never think of again."

Cilla walks up to the counter to get a refill on her coffee, so Sienna leans forward and whispers, "Don't worry. We'll take care of it. But I have to know. Who is this boyfriend of yours?"

I can't tell her Ian's real name, so instead I give her his pen name. "T. Anderson."

Her eyes grow wide with surprise, and the look of shock on her face tells me she's heard of him and our book. "Do you mean to tell me you're sleeping with the author of Silk? I picked it up after you mentioned it in that interview. Oh my God, Kristina! It's so fucking hot!"

Blushing, I smile, knowing exactly how hot our story is. "I know. I'm his muse, and it's about us, basically."

"I have to know! Is he as hot in person as the male character is in the book? The things Sean does to Kate—oh my everloving God! I want a man who does that to me."

I hear Cilla behind us, so I say, "Shhh. I don't want anyone to know."

She sits down and I know instantly she heard something. "Don't want anyone to know what? Tell me."

Sienna quickly changes the subject and asks her, "So what exactly do you have to do with The Creeper to get out of financial ruin?"

"Don't try to get me talking about him. I want to know who Kristina's new boyfriend is."

It's only a fake name, so I say, "His name is T. Anderson. But don't tell anyone because we want to keep our privacy, okay?"

"Okay, but who is this guy? You say his name like I should know."

"He's nobody, Cilla," I say as Sienna shoots me a look across the table to tell me we're in the clear. "Just a guy who's dating an actress."

She takes a sip of her fresh coffee and shrugs. "Then he better get used to the idea that privacy is a thing of the past. I told you a while back. It's the age of TMZ, Kristina. Privacy is so last century."

Sienna thankfully distracts her from my problems with her opinion on The Creeper, and for the first time today I'm not terrified what I have with Ian is going to be ruined by two little nights with Gavin. All I have to do is convince him that neither of our careers will benefit from anyone finding out. He's got a good thing going with the women he parades around town, a different one to each party and premier, so he'll probably agree that our little tryst should stay our little secret.

At least I hope he does.

CHAPTER SEVEN

Ian

THE SOBER AND drug-free version of me writes even better than before I find out after realizing I've written an entire chapter by the time I need to begin getting dinner ready. Sitting back in my chair, I fold my arms behind my head, pleased with how Silk and Steel is already coming. I'd never planned a sequel since I'd never planned on much happening with the first book, but now that I'm back and into the story, I can honestly say I've never been happier writing any book.

Or happier in general. That's all because of Kristina.

I know I still have a lot of making up to do to her. A few weeks in rehab and a reunion of mind-blowing sex is a good start, but certainly not the end. She deserves so much more, and now that I'm clean, I intend of doing everything in my power to give it to her.

Starting with a romantic candlelit dinner of

my world famous risotto and then another night of incredible sex. After that, I'm thinking I will spend the rest of my life showing her how much I love her and how I don't want to live without her.

I may be clean and sober, but the part of me that's susceptible to addiction hasn't gone away, and now my only addiction is Kristina.

As far as addictions go, she's a pretty fantastic one.

My email alert dings to let me know I have a new message in my inbox, and I open up an email from an agent who's tried to contact me three times since Silk hit the bestseller lists. This morning when I deleted all but the most urgent emails that I'd missed while I was gone to rehab, hers and those from two other agents and even some movie producer had gone into the trash, along with scores of spam emails about how I could increase the size of my penis and offers from some Irish lottery commission that seems to want to send me some winnings I had no idea about.

But now as I read her fourth email, I wonder if I should consider at least speaking to her about the potential for Silk concerning New York and foreign rights. I certainly don't have time to be dealing with those issues, and if there's money to be made, I'd eventually need an agent to handle the contracts. I'd thought about asking Sheila, but as I told Kristina, she doesn't rep erotica or romance authors of any type, self-published or New York.

Dinner's more important, though, so business will have to wait. Shutting my laptop, I head into the kitchen to make the best goddamned risotto I've ever created and wait for the woman I love.

KRISTINA STANDS BEHIND me watching as I slowly add the chicken stock and stir until each ladle-full is absorbed. Turning around, I wink at her. "Now you know the secret to the world's best risotto. You have to make sure to use Arborio rice and add the stock slowly. And you need to stir constantly."

She leans her chin on my shoulder and kisses me on the neck. "The world's best risotto made by the world's best guy. How long until we eat? I'm starving and this smells fantastic."

I add the final ladle of stock and continue stirring it into the rice. "A few more minutes. Not too long."

Her hands slide down my sides, and she hugs me to her, purring in my ear, "I have an idea of what we could be doing instead of all this stirring."

Turning my head, I kiss her softly, but her kiss quickly turns into something far more erotic, and for a moment I completely forget about the risotto until I feel the rice begin to stick to the bottom of the pan.

I reluctantly break the kiss, wishing dinner was done already. "Great food calls. We'll pick that up right where we left off as soon as we finish dinner."

She moans sweetly in my ear, "I want you to know I'm pouting, Ian."

I look and see her mouth turned down in an adorable pout. "I promise not too long and then once we have a dinner of this delicious risotto, I'm going to fuck you slow and easy right there in front of those windows and give our friend the show of his life."

"Yes," she moans as her hands travel down to the front of my pants. Palming my hard cock through the fabric, she says, "But I might not be able to wait for slow and easy. I might need you to fuck me hard and fast. Is that okay?"

My stirring speeds up as she strokes me from balls to tip, and for a moment I can't think of anything but being buried inside her tight cunt. Only when she moves her hand away am I able to think clearly again, and I look down to see the risotto is finally done.

"Dinner is served," I announce, barely able to keep my calm as my cock demands what Kristina is offering.

I scoop the food onto our plates and sit down, prepared to eat, but Kristina has different plans. Straddling me, she lowers herself onto my lap as her skirt rides up to show the milky white skin at the tops of her thighs. In my ear, she whispers, "Dinner is lovely, but I'm hungry for something else."

Her tongue softly glides over the shell of my ear, sending jolts of excitement through my body as she unbuttons my shirt and whispers how much she wants me to fuck her while she undoes each button.

I run my hands over the tops of those gorgeous thighs, slipping my thumbs under her skirt to feel her smooth pussy. She's not wearing anything under her clothes, so once I remove them, she's there sitting on my lap, naked and mine to do with as I please.

My cock already aches from being so hard, so by the time she takes it out of my pants, I'm ready for her and not as interested anymore in taking it easy.

"I'm not sure I can do slow right now," I say looking up at her as she stares at my cock and licks her lips.

"I don't want slow, Ian. I want wild and desperate. I want anyone who sees me after this to know your cock owned me. I want it to be obvious I'm yours."

Her words and the way she says them in her soft, seductive voice make my head spin. My hand on the back of her neck, I pull her mouth down to mine and kiss her hard, my tongue snaking in over her lips to find her tongue. My fingers find her pussy drenched and needy for me, and she moans as I slide two into her slick cunt.

"Fuck me, please. Hurry. I need to feel you inside me."

I grab her by the hips and position her over my cock ready for her. Looking up at her, I watch her squeeze her nipples, her eyes closed as she waits for me to lower her down onto me.

I don't want slow anymore either.

"Open your eyes, Kristina," I order and see her eyelids fly open. "I want you to watch when my cock slams into that pretty cunt of yours."

She bites her pouty lower lip and nods. "Yes. Do it. I need it."

Reaching up, I cup one of her perfect breasts and squeeze the deep pink nipple hard like I know she loves. "Harder?"

She rolls her hips so her pussy glides over my shaft and moans softly, "Yes."

I pinch her nipple between my thumb and forefinger and see the pain register on her face, but she doesn't want me to let up, so I do the same to the other nipple and watch as her mouth gently hangs open in ecstasy.

"Ride my cock, baby. Let me see you take it all."

My hands leave those gorgeous breasts to take their places on her hips, and I slam her down onto me, loving the vision of my cock disappearing into her body. I guide her pace, pushing her off me and then back down over and over. She rides me with abandon while I watch her, falling in love more every minute.

As she moves closer to her orgasm, she leans forward and kisses me like my lips possess everything she desires. Stuffing my hands into her hair, I close my fists and tug hard, loving the feel of her fucking me.

"I'm close," she groans against my lips. "So close."

I tilt my hips slightly so my cock glides over her G-spot and see that's all it takes. Her walls close in around my cock, squeezing it, and she comes hard as her hips buck against me and her mouth plunders mine. She's raw and so entirely feminine at that moment, and I love that I could give her this.

As her body slows from her release, she says quietly, "You didn't come. Why?"

I know what she's thinking. She's worried it's like the last time I couldn't get off because of the drugs. Smiling, I shake my head. "I was so engrossed with wanting you to come that I couldn't think of anything else."

"Oh. I worried…" Her sentence hangs in the air unfinished, but I know what she was worried about.

"No. Nothing like that. Just me watching you and loving what I see."

A tiny smile forms on that mouth I love, and she asks, "Anything else you like watching?"

I know what she means, and yes, I love watching her go down on me. She lifts herself off me and lowers to her knees. Pushing her hair back, I gaze down at her beautiful face. "I love when you suck me off, Kristina."

She runs her hand up my slick cock and licks her lips. "Only you."

I try to keep my eyes open as she slides the head into her warm mouth, but the feeling of her tongue dancing over my skin takes my breath away and I lean back to enjoy my first blowjob since leaving for rehab. All sexual positions are good, but there's nothing like a woman you adore sucking your cock and swallowing everything you give her.

Kristina lavishes attention on my cock like it's

an eight inch god she worships. With every time she takes me in as far as she can go, she looks up at me with a mixture of innocence and seduction that only intensifies the experience. She's madonna and whore all in one.

And all mine.

I watch as she lets my cock pop playfully out of her mouth before she lowers her mouth to the very base to plant a kiss as she cups my balls to give them a gentle squeeze. Then she runs the tip of her tongue up the underside of my shaft, nearly taking the top of my head off, and as she reaches the swollen crown she whispers sweetly, "Is my man ready to come?"

More than ready. A few minutes more of this and I might not be able to walk until morning.

Jamming my hands into her hair, I tug her head down onto my cock so all of me is in her mouth. The tip hits the back of her throat, making her gag a little, so I lift her a few inches and say, "Suck me dry."

She does just as I command and sucks my cock like only she can. That mixture of innocence and experience melds into a blowjob better than any she's ever given me, and when I flood her mouth, she takes every drop I have to give.

And when she lifts her head to let me slip out of her mouth one last time, her smile shows me I wasn't the only one who enjoyed myself.

I pull her up onto my lap but not to fuck her again. This time I just want to hold her and tell her how much I love her. She curls up against me and whispers, "I know we had our reunion yesterday, but I just wanted to say I missed you so much when you were gone."

There's a sadness in her voice from how lonely I know she was, and I hate that I'm the reason that's there. I place a kiss on the top of her head and tell her the truth. "I never meant to hurt you, Kristina. I swear I didn't."

She shakes her head against my chest and wraps her arms around me. "You don't have to apologize. You didn't mean to hurt me. I understand now. Sometimes when you're in love you do things and when you see they hurt the person you care for, it hurts you too."

"I promise no more hurting because of that. I promise."

Looking up at me, she gives me a gentle smile and nods. "We might as well get to this dinner you made. It's probably cold by now."

"We'll just heat it up. And when we're done, I want to tell you all the news about Silk."

Kristina sits up straight on me and knits her brows. "News? Something else happened?"

I kiss the tip of her nose. "I promise to tell

you everything after dinner, but I'll give one hint. How would the role of Kate Silk sound?"

Her eyes get big as her mouth drops open. "Role? Is someone thinking of making a film of your book?"

"Our book and no more details until we eat, so we better get moving."

She hurriedly puts on some of her clothes as I slip my satisfied cock back inside my pants, and even as we eat dinner, she can't help but ask to hear more about my details concerning Silk. I hold off telling her, wanting to wait until we're settled in on the couch in each other's arms to tell her about all the interest in our story.

"PLEASE TELL ME now, Ian. I'm so excited to hear about all of this," Kristina says eagerly as she cuddles up next to me on my leather couch.

I run my fingers over the ends of her hair as I explain about the emails I've received from agents, publishers, and the producer all interested in Silk. As thrilled as I knew she'd be, she's all smiles at the idea that what began with just the two of us could become something so much bigger.

Resting her head on my shoulder, she looks up with curious eyes and asks, "So what are you going to do?"

"You mean what are we going to do. It's our

story, Kristina. You're my muse, and Silk wouldn't exist without you."

"I didn't do anything, Ian. You wrote this story. This is your talent they love. Your story people are talking about. I'm just a character in the book you crafted."

I shake my head at how wrong she is. "Ian Anwell writes historical fiction. He writes it pretty well too. But T. Anderson only writes when you're with him. All those weeks we weren't together and every time we've been apart even for a few days, I didn't write a word. I couldn't. Silk is our story. Without you, there is no story."

"I read it, you know. The day before you came back," she says shyly.

"What did you think?"

"It's so full of passion and love. Is that how you see us?"

"Of course. I love you."

She lowers her head. "I love you too, but I didn't realize how much you felt for me early on."

I tip her head back and kiss her softly. "From practically the moment we met. And before that I was already addicted to you."

"Another addiction," she says sadly.

"A good one, though. Being addicted to you has never hurt me."

Shaking her head, she frowns. "That's not

true. There's Rome and when I ran away from you that first time. And..."

"And what? None of that was you hurting me intentionally. I know that."

She buries her head in my chest and mumbles, "I'm so sorry, Ian. I've done such awful things because I'm so stupid."

I try to get her to look at me, but she won't budge. I kiss the top of her head and say in her ear, "You didn't do anything stupid or awful. It's okay. Why don't I tell you what I was thinking about for a Silk film? I bet that will make you happy."

Kristina lifts her head, and I see she's crying. Wiping her tear-stained cheek, she sobs, "I'm not unhappy, Ian. I just regret the things I've done to hurt you."

I cradle her face in my hands and try to kiss her worries away. "You didn't hurt me. What do you think about you starring in the film, if it's ever made? I can't imagine another actress ever being able to play Kate Silk as well as the woman she's based on."

"Me? Do you think that could ever happen?" she asks in amazement.

"I won't have it any other way. It's you or no one, Kristina. There are also agents looking to talk to me about taking the book to a New York publisher too."

"Do you want to do that? Won't that be a problem with your books?"

"It might be, so I have to think long and hard about what to do. I won't do anything without your input, though."

"As long as you're happy, I'm happy. That's all that matters to me, Ian."

I pull her close and nuzzle her neck. "You know what else? I'm going to include what we just did before dinner in Silk and Steel."

For the first time since she arrived tonight, I hear her giggle. Leaning back, I see a blush cover her cheeks at the mention of me writing that scene, and I can't help but be charmed. For as uninhibited as she is when we make love, she's still that sweet, bashful woman I met in Jax's.

And I love both the madonna part and the whore part to her equally.

CHAPTER EIGHT

Kristina

FOUR DAYS OF complete and total bliss, most of them spent in Ian's arms, have made me feel like everything in my life had turned around. My role in Original Sin has made me realize it was time for me to spread my wings and try meatier parts. Gavin has been perfectly agreeable to keeping our dalliance private as the relationship he's begun with another of our co-stars is taking off and he doesn't want to ruin his chances with her.

And best of all, Ian and I are happier than I thought two people possibly could be. The bumps in the road to this point tested us, but we've come out stronger on the other side, and I couldn't be more in love.

Life is truly good and getting better every day.

Ian moans softly in his sleep as he rolls over to lay his head on my shoulder. His scruffy beard scratches my skin, but I don't care if he forgets to shave again today like he did yesterday. Spending all day in bed leads to that, even if we did move to the shower for a while before returning to right here to spend the night, him writing and me watching him.

I never thought sitting next to someone as they write could be so interesting. He chooses every word so carefully, just like when he speaks, so that the end result is entirely magical to the ear and the eye. Under his care, the characters come to life as he gives them terrible obstacles and forces them to make heartbreaking choices, but I know in the end Kate and Sean will end up happy, just like Ian and me.

I watch him as he sleeps so contented and like to believe that I'm a big reason why he no longer tosses and turns like he used to. I fell in love with a man who will forever struggle with addiction, and I want to be the one he can't shake.

Maybe that's selfish. Maybe it's something I should be ashamed of because I want him to not be able to live without me like I can't without him.

I don't care if it is and I won't be ashamed of wanting the kind of love he gives me. Some love is worth it.

His hand rests heavily on my stomach, trapping me there next to him as he sleeps, but in truth, there's nowhere else in the world I'd rather be. I lightly trace the outline of his long fingers, noting how strong they feel even when they aren't holding me or balled into a sensual fist as he tugs at my hair in the heat of passion.

My finger glides up over his over arm, toned and lean, to his shoulder, and I stop as I reach his collarbone, afraid if I continue I'll wake him. I could lie here forever just studying him and be perfectly happy.

The only thing that would make me happier is to hear him tell me he loves me or say something sexy in his special way only he can do, his words so perfectly chosen that they can excite me without him even touching my body.

His dark hair hangs over the left side of his face, hiding his chiseled cheekbone and eye with its long lashes. I want to reach out and run my fingertip down the bridge of his nose so straight and perfect. He's so beautiful lying there peacefully beside me as if all his demons have been slayed and what's left is the man I've adored from that first night we met.

For the first time with a man, I feel like tomorrow will be okay.

I lean over to kiss the top of his head, loving the silky feel of his hair against my lips. Inhaling deeply, I smell the light coconut and vanilla scent from the shampoo I used to wash his hair yesterday afternoon. It's warm and sensual like him, and forever it will remind me of standing in the shower with the water pouring over us and me working hard to convince him to let me use my shampoo on his hair instead of his old ordinary brand and him finally giving me a crooked smile and saying, "I can't refuse you anything, so go ahead. Do your worst."

As I reminisce about the sex that followed, my phone vibrates in my purse nearby on the floor. Looking over at Ian's nightstand, I see the clock says it's just after nine. That's entirely too early for anyone to be texting me. I ignore it and return to enjoying the thought of Ian making love to me. Texting before ten in the morning is just rude.

But my phone vibrates again two minutes later. And then three minutes after that. Whoever it is doesn't understand phone etiquette, so I try to ignore the almost constant vibrating noise coming from my purse. But by the time ten texts have come in, I begin to worry that it isn't just rudeness on someone's part but a real emergency.

Easing my arm out from underneath Ian's head, I reach for my purse and grab my phone. I swipe the screen and there in front of me I see the reason my phone is blowing up.

The one thing I dreaded more than anything

else in the world has happened. Somehow, the tabloids have found out what happened in Vancouver and they're announcing it like it's a goddamned gold rush.

> *Kristina, the celebrity gossip site All The Dirt is running a story about you and Gavin Somers in Vancouver saying you cheated on your boyfriend! Who the fuck is your boyfriend? Is this serious? Why do they think this is a huge story? Call me ASAP!*

Joanne's text makes my stomach clench in terror. Is the story already live? I scramble to figure out when her message came in. 9:01. And it's 9:20 already!

Another text comes in, this one from my agent. Her fourth text of the morning tells me she's confused and frightened. I know exactly how she feels.

> *Joanne hasn't stopped texting me about whatever you did in Vancouver and some boyfriend here. What's happening? What is this about? Are you okay?*

No. I'm definitely not okay. I look over at Ian still sleeping peacefully as everything else in my world is crashing down around my ears. All I want is to have him hold me and tell me everything will be okay, and he's the only person I can't look to for help now.

Oh, God. What am I going to do? When he finds out what happened with Gavin, he's never going to forgive me. Why would he? He was battling his demons in that rehab center and I couldn't even stay loyal and stand by him.

I'd leave me too.

No! I couldn't let that happen. I had to find a way to fix this before he found out. I couldn't let him be hurt this way.

Another text from my agent makes my blood run cold. *Is T. Anderson really the author Ian Anwell? Why aren't you calling me? Call me now!*

Oh my God! How did they find out?

I need to see this story, so I quickly find All The Dirt's website on my phone and read through the story as my heart pounds frantically in my chest. The title of the article is awful, and it only gets worse from there. Somehow they know everything.

How could they have found out?

Two Timing 'Tina

All The Dirt hears that actress Kristina Richards has been very busy lately. First she was seen kanoodling with her co-star in Original Sin Gavin Somers while they were shooting in Vancouver recently, and as you can see by the picture below, they were just as cozy as two people could be. Our source reports that cuddling in a restaurant booth isn't all they were up to either.

But now we here at All The Dirt hear that while she was getting hot and heavy with Gavin, her boyfriend, author Ian Anwell, was off at rehab again trying to shake his drug habit for the fifth time. So he was trying to clean up and she was getting down and dirty.

And what might be the biggest news of all?

Sources confirm that Ian Anwell, bestselling author of the historical fiction books Caligula's Dream and Nero's Nightmare is, in fact, T. Anderson, the author of the book that's on everyone's ereader this year, Silk!

Two timing 'Tina has been very busy indeed! But the question now is: How will her boyfriend handle the news of her infidelity?

I feel like I'm going to throw up. When Ian finds out I not only cheated on him when he was in the fight of his life but also that the world knows he's really T. Anderson and the author of an erotic book, he'll never forgive me.

My mind spins with what to do. I can't tell

him. I don't know how. Maybe I can get Joanne to get that website to retract the article.

But why would they? Nothing they wrote is false. Probably a first for them.

The walls of Ian's apartment begin to feel like they're closing in on me. I need to get out of here and figure out what to do. Silently, I get out of bed and dress to leave.

To run away. In truth, that's what I'm doing.

As I turn to leave, I look at his serene face as he sleeps and choke up as tears well up in my eyes. I don't want to go, but I need to see if I can fix the damage I've caused before he gets hurt.

Who am I kidding? He's already been hurt. I can only pray that when the world finds out he's really T. Anderson that what he's feared all along won't happen. If his publisher and readers turn on his historical books, I won't be able to forgive myself.

I'm sorry, Ian. I never meant for any of this to happen.

✧   ✧   ✧

"Sienna, please tell me you didn't sell the details of my life to that All The Dirt website."

I see by the shock in her expression that she genuinely doesn't know what I'm talking about. I didn't think it was her, but I had to ask. Sagging against the wall outside her door, I hang my head. "I'm sorry. I never thought you'd really do that to me."

"Kristina, come inside and tell me what the hell is going on."

She takes my hand and drags me in as I begin to explain everything that's happened that morning. By the time I reach the part about my dating Ian and his secret pen name being revealed, her mouth is hanging open in shock.

"Oh my God, honey! What are you going to do?"

As I practically collapse onto her loveseat, I shake my head, trying to hold back the tears. "I don't know. And I don't know which is worse—Ian finding out I cheated on him with Gavin while he was in rehab or his secret out for everyone to see?"

Sienna gives my hand a sympathetic squeeze, but I can see in her eyes how awful even she thinks this is.

"Okay, what's the worst that can happen?"

My heart skips a beat as the thought of what the worst truly is tears through my brain. "Ian never forgiving me for betraying him not just once, but twice. Me losing the man I love."

"Okay. Well, is there any way you or your people can get this story killed?"

I shake my head. "No. They didn't report anything false, so I don't have a leg to stand on. And it doesn't matter anyway if they did. It's out there already."

"How did this happen, Kristina? Who did you tell other than me?"

"I only told you that day at the café." Then the truth hits me. Cilla. "Oh my God! Cilla sold her story to that rag site for money, didn't she?" I ask in horror as the reality of it settles into my mind.

For a moment, Sienna can't believe it, but it's the only thing that makes sense. "I can't believe that, Kristina. Cilla's a lot of things, but she's wouldn't do this to you."

"She would if she was desperate for money, which is exactly what she is if she's back with her ex-husband. She sold the details she'd heard that day to All The Dirt and now my life is ruined."

"Oh, honey. I'm so sorry. I brought her that day. I'm to blame."

"No, you're not. This is my fault. I cheated on him."

"But how did they find out Ian's really T. Anderson? You never told me that, so Cilla couldn't have overheard it."

I close my eyes and lean my head back against the cushion. "I have no idea. I never told anyone, so they must have found out on their own."

"What are you going to do? You can't just wait for him to find out on his own, Kristina. You just left him there in his apartment without even telling him you were leaving?"

Barely holding back the tears, I hide my face in my hands. "I didn't know what to do, so I ran, like I always do when I get scared. My publicist and my agent have been texting me like mad all morning, but I don't know what to say to them either. None of it's untrue, so what's the point?"

She wraps her arm around me, and I finally let it all out, unable to keep my sadness in anymore. I've lost the one person I love more than anyone in this world and when everyone finds out his secret, he'll be ruined.

"Oh, honey. I know it seems bad now, but things have a way of working out. It sounds clichéd, but they do. If it's true love, you guys will be able to overcome this."

Looking up, I dry my eyes. "That's pretty optimistic of you, Sienna. I had no idea you were such a romantic. But what if it wasn't true love but love just the same? I don't want to lose him."

She shakes her head and frowns. "I don't know then. I guess all you can do is hope he can forgive you."

"I have to figure out how I'm going to tell

him what I've done. I better get going."

"Okay, but call me if you need anything. While you're dealing with that, I'm going to find Cilla and rip her a new one for being such a two-faced bitch."

I know Sienna means well, but even the idea of her tearing into Cilla for being the worst friend in the world can't cheer me up now. I'm going to have to fight for Ian with everything I have inside me, but what if he doesn't want me anymore?

What if he can't forgive me?

As the cab turns the corner toward Ian's building, I see the crowd of photographers and media gathered in front, and I know my problems have just gotten a hundred times worse. If they're waiting for him, the news has spread about who he really is and he has no idea.

The cabbie looks back at me in the rearview mirror. "Looks like they're onto someone famous here. You still want to get out or should I take you somewhere else?"

We slowly roll by the chaotic scene outside Ian's building, and I look up at his living room windows wishing I was up there with him hidden away from all the madness that's about to descend upon us, all because of me. Nodding toward the cabbie still staring back at me, I give him my address instead and sink into the seat to avoid the prying eyes of the media now stalking the man I love.

I take one last look back as we turn the corner and hope to God I haven't spent my last night there with Ian. I have to find some way to convince him he should forgive me. I can't let this ruin the best thing in my life.

CHAPTER NINE

Ian

I STRETCH THE sleep from my limbs and open my eyes to see I'm alone in bed. Still tired, I roll over and wait for Kristina to return and cuddle up next to me. Looking at the clock, I see it's close to ten. I've got a full day of writing planned, but another hour or so in bed won't hurt.

The sound of my cell phone ringing wakes me up and I open my eyes to see it's nearly noon. Turning my head, I see Kristina's side of the bed empty. I wonder where she is, but she's probably in the bathroom getting ready for the day. My phone thankfully stops ringing, but starts up again almost immediately. Still groggy, I answer my phone more concerned with why I slept so late than whoever is calling me.

"Hello?" I mumble as I work to focus my still bleary eyes.

"Ian? What are you doing?"

I vaguely recognize my agent's voice, but it sounds frantic. Definitely not what a person wants to hear first thing in the morning. "Sheila, I just woke up, but don't worry. I'm not back to doing anything bad. I just overslept today."

"You overslept? So you don't know about what's happened?" she asks, her voice in full panic mode.

"No. Did something happen?" I ask, wide awake and beginning to get worried myself. Sheila isn't the kind of woman to go off the deep end, and if she's upset about something, it must be big.

"Oh, Ian. Just when I thought you got lucky, it's all a mess. I don't believe most of it. I can't, but you need to wake up and listen to me."

I sit up and swing my legs off the bed. "Sheila, calm down. Whatever it is, I'll be fine. Just tell me what's going on and we'll handle it."

"Are you alone?"

"No." I begin to walk through the apartment and I don't see Kristina anywhere. "Well, maybe. I think Kristina must have run out for something. What does it matter if I'm alone or not, though?"

"Ian, what did you do when you went to Rome, other than drugs? Did you even research for the Marc Antony book, or was that all a lie?"

I've never felt more confused than I do at that moment. I don't know where Kristina is and nothing Sheila's saying is making sense. Leaning back against the kitchen counter, I try to clear my head, but her questions sound like madness.

"I admit I went back to doing heroin on my trip to Rome, but I spent the time researching, Sheila. What's all this about?"

"Who is T. Anderson, Ian?"

My eyes fly open wide at her mention of the pen name only Kristina and I know about. My mind begins spinning out of control as she continues to ask who T. Anderson is and if I've secretly written a book without her knowing.

"How did you find out?"

"It's all over the news, Ian! So it's true? How could you do this? I'm your agent and you kept this from me?"

"What do you mean it's all over the news?" I ask as I begin to panic like she is. "What news?"

"The gossip website All The Dirt posted an article about you being this author and being in rehab this last time. It will be on Page Six by tomorrow."

"It's not that big a deal, Sheila. I wrote a book and published it on my own. It did better than I thought it ever would, but I'm not planning on throwing away my career writing historical fiction as Ian Anwell. Somebody must have made the connection, but the two have nothing to do with one another."

Sheila is silent for a long moment and then says quietly, "It's not that easy, Ian. Those two genres don't complement each other."

"Don't worry. It was just something that came about as a result of me meeting Kristina. I don't plan on writing many more as T. Anderson, so you won't lose me."

"It's much worse than you think. Right now, your publisher is telling me that the Marc Antony project is on hold, and I'm hearing the same thing for the film of Caligula's Dream."

"Why? Does it really matter what I do under a pen name?"

"If no one had found out, it wouldn't matter, but now that people know Ian Anwell wrote Silk, you're too sexy for historical fiction."

Now I'm in full panic mode like she was a few minutes ago. "What are you saying? That my career is ruined because I wrote one erotic book? That's fucking crazy."

"Ian, I'll do what I can, but for right now, you're just not a name they want to be associated with. But there's more."

More? Like what? Do they plan to put me in the stockade in the public square for having impure thoughts?

Suddenly, the room feels like it's spinning out

of control. As she begins to read from the All The Dirt post, I stumble to the table and fall into a chair. I can't believe what I'm hearing.

"Honey, I'm so sorry, but they said this about Kristina. 'All The Dirt hears that actress Kristina Richards has been very busy lately. First she was seen kanoodling with her co-star in Original Sin Gavin Somers while they were shooting in Vancouver recently, and as you can see by the picture below, they were just as cozy as two people could be. Our source reports that cuddling in a restaurant booth isn't all they were up to either.

But now we here at All The Dirt hear that while she was getting hot and heavy with Gavin, her boyfriend author Ian Anwell was off at rehab again trying to shake his drug habit for the fifth time. So he was trying to clean up and she was getting down and dirty.'"

I close my eyes as the bile begins to rise in my throat. "No. No. They're a gossip site. They got this one wrong, though. She wasn't with anyone."

Even as I defend her, I can't help but replay every moment together since I returned and every word she wrote me in those letters she sent all the while I was in rehab. Is it possible? Did she go with that guy while I was spending time getting clean so we could have a life together?

"I'm sure you're right, Ian. She clearly loves

you. I saw that the night I took you to Meadowbrook."

"Yeah, these sites get shit wrong all the time, Sheila. They aren't wrong about me being T. Anderson or about Silk. I did write it," I say, working to keep my voice from shaking I'm so upset. "But if you want, I'll make it up to you for keeping it secret by letting you be my agent for it. I've had a few contact me already, in addition to a film producer interested in talking about making a movie of the story."

"I don't usually work with that genre, but for you, I'll see what I can do. Don't worry. I'll handle everything else too. I think for the time being you might want to lay low, though. This is a story the media thinks has legs with the pen name, the popularity of Silk, and the whole cheating story."

"She didn't cheat, Sheila."

"Okay, but they don't know that, so this story seems like it has all the elements the media likes. I think until everything dies down, you should go away for a little while. Take Kristina and leave as soon as you can. You still have that cabin upstate. Go there. Sit in front of a roaring fire and lay low until I can clear things up here."

I hate the idea of running away and hiding, but she's right. Staying in the city won't help matters.

"Okay, I need a little time off anyway. I'll give you a call in a few days."

"Sounds good, Ian. Don't worry. I'll handle things for you like I always have. You don't have to worry about this. Go enjoy a little R and R with Kristina."

I hear the sympathy in her voice, but it's not for what's happened to my writing career. She thinks the part of the story about Kristina is true.

And with every minute that passes, I begin to think it is too.

I LOOK AROUND my apartment where just twelve hours earlier we were happier than we'd ever been before. For four days we'd enjoyed just being with one another in the way two people in love did. Completely and sublimely in love. Now all this place feels is empty. I don't know where she is or why she left. Did she leave because this story went public and it's true?

Flipping open my laptop, I make my way to the All The Dirt website and read the post, unable to stop myself from looking at the picture of her with this guy Gavin she worked with on that film in Vancouver.

Brown hair, average build, nothing to make him noteworthy. Goofy too perfect smile. And I hate him because there she is in his arms smiling like I thought she only smiled for me.

I don't want to believe she betrayed me so completely. I don't want to believe she cheated on me with this guy and then broke her promise to me and told the world about T. Anderson and our story.

I don't, but I can't help it. Every moment that goes by without a word from her tells me I need to begin believing it.

I can't handle this. It hurts too much. I need something to help me deal with this.

Rummaging through my kitchen cabinets for anything to help me take the edge off how bad I feel, I find a bottle of whisky somebody gave me for Christmas one year. The stuff's shit, but right now, I don't care if it's fucking lighter fluid.

I just need to be something other than sober.

I pour myself a glass and down it fast, hoping it hits me and dulls the pain that's already beginning to hurt too fucking much. Another one goes down just as quick and begins to do the job.

By the third glass, my rage and hurt have subsided enough for me to at least try to understand what happened, so I call Kristina but get no answer. I wait ten minutes for her to call me back, finishing my drink and pouring myself another, but my phone doesn't make a sound.

Finally, I text her and pray to God she answers with something that doesn't make me feel even worse than I already do.

I read the All The Dirt post. All I want to know is if it's true.

Waiting for my phone to vibrate, I try to remember any happy moment between us, but they're all blocked by the sick feeling I have that she betrayed me.

Her message comes in, and for a moment a feeling of dread washes over me. I can't put off looking at it, though, so after waiting a minute, I pick it up and read her text, my heart slamming against my chest as the words flow by my eyes.

I never told anyone about our story or that you wrote it, Ian. I wouldn't do that to you. I love you. I wouldn't ruin your life like that.

My hands shake as I write the text that may be the end of all the happiness I've ever wanted.

Did you sleep with him while I was in rehab?

Her message takes too long, and I know the answer before my phone even tells me she's texted back. When it vibrates against the top of the table where we ate every meal together, I feel empty, like someone's carved out my insides and left me hollow. I look down and read the words that tear my heart out.

Yes but it was nothing. I'm coming there right now and we'll talk. I can explain everything, Ian. I love you. Please believe me. I can explain.

As the truth of what she did becomes reality in my mind, I stand from the table and grab a bag to fill with things I'll need up at the cabin. I can't stay here and listen to the woman I love tell me the reasons why she slept with another man while I was in rehab missing her more than I'd ever missed anyone in my life.

I reach the lobby and see the doorman just as I notice the mob of photographers standing outside the front door. He recognizes me immediately and steps in front of me to shield me from them.

"Mr. Anwell, I think we should find another way for you to exit the building today."

"Good idea. I'm going to be driving, so I just need to get down to the garage." He seems to study me for a long moment, and I realize I probably reek of cheap whisky, so I add, "I'm fine. No need to worry."

"Yes, sir." Extending his arm, he guides me to the door to the garage, never moving from in front of me. "Drive safely, sir."

I head past him toward my parking spot where my BMW Series 6 is parked and smile. "Thanks."

"Do you have any instructions in case Miss Richards arrives tonight while they're still here?"

Shaking my head, I try to keep the sadness I'm feeling over losing her from my voice. "Nope. She's used to that kind of thing. She'll be fine."

"Yes, sir. Drive safely."

Driving safely is likely not going to happen since I'm pretty fucking buzzed from the cheap Christmas gift booze, so I speed out of the parking garage and head up the street, blowing the horn at the photographer vultures as I pass. For a few minutes I don't feel like I've lost everything I love and I'm all alone, but that doesn't last and as roar up the road to my cabin upstate, all I feel is empty.

Empty and lost without her.

IAN AND KRISTINA'S STORY
CONCLUDES IN CLAIM (ADDICTED TO
YOU #4)
GET YOUR COPY TODAY!

IF I DREAM (CORRUPTED LOVE #1)

A story of passion, crime, and the lengths you go to for love…

If I dream, will you dare?

Ryder
All I wanted was my freedom. It's all I'd dreamed of from the first time I stood in the ring. Until I entered Robert Erickson's world. Until Serena. Cruelty and ugliness surrounded me, but she was beautiful and good. I wanted to protect her from her father's world, even though I knew being with her could mean the end of me.

Serena
I wanted for nothing as the daughter of one of the richest men in the world. But all my father's money couldn't buy what I truly craved. Until Ryder. I wanted all he was, all he brought out in me. All he made me desire.

Our love was forbidden by the one person who had the power to harm us. We dreamed of more than living in that world, though. We dreamed of having it all, but did we dare?

CHAPTER ONE

Ryder

A S USUAL, THE crowd at The Pit screamed its lust for the two of us to pound the fuck out of each other. Impatient bastards. I couldn't hear any one person's words clearly, but I'd done this enough times to know what the people who'd come to watch us wanted.

Blood. Pain. And one of us as close to death as possible. It thrilled them in some sick way almost as much as I suspected winning did when their fighter crushed another person.

My opponent tonight stood nearly as tall as I did at six foot three, but his body was smaller than mine. He looked older, like something in the way he carried himself said he'd seen more of life than I had. His angular face looked hard, and on either side of his perfectly straight nose were eyes staring me down like he thought squinting and grimacing would make me run for the nearest exit like some fucking scared little boy. He was fighting the wrong person if that's what he expected.

I'd never lost and for good reason. When you had nothing but the feel of your fists beating the hell out of someone and the sound of those rabid fucks cheering you on like you were some kind of hero for nearly killing another man, all you wanted was to win.

Fifteen times I'd won right here in this dank warehouse against guys bigger and stronger than me, and every time it seemed to surprise everyone. Even those who had bet on me.

If they only knew how unlikely it was anyone could match the rage inside me, they'd never bet against me again.

Some impatient bastard behind me barked, "Stop dancing around! Hit 'em!"

Mr. Grimace narrowed his eyes until he could barely see out of them and took a deep breath. Why did he bother with all this tough guy bullshit? That's not what these bloodthirsty fucks wanted.

Pain is what they wanted.

So that's what they'd get. His or mine. It didn't matter to them.

"Scared, motherfucker?" he grunted out in a deep voice I knew wasn't really how he talked. "I'm going to fuck you up."

I didn't bother answering.

He caught me in the face with a hard right that scrambled my brains for a second, and then his fist skidded along my jaw and ran square into my right shoulder. The last guy I fought had done a number on that one, so that hurt like a bitch.

I knew how this went, though. The people around us wanted a show as much as they wanted a fight. I could have just beat the fuck out of him and won, but that's not what this was. I'd been told that enough times to understand even if I could pound the piss out of a guy, I had to at least make it look like a fight and not just some sad beat down.

So that's what I did. I took a few hits, sometimes more than a few, and let it look like there was some chance I wouldn't win. The other guy got to feel pretty big in the shorts and the crowd got to feel like this was really a match between two fighters.

It wasn't, though.

He paraded around like a peacock, preening to the crowd while I gritted my teeth and pushed my shoulder back into place. I took a deep breath and waited for the moment I'd show him who he was dealing with.

Flush with the love of the crowd, he turned back to face me. A few shots into me had made him think he had a chance.

I stepped forward as he lunged at me and leveled my fist against his jaw. His head ricocheted back, sending him reeling for a second or two, but I didn't let up. My right hand zeroed in on his face again, this time connecting with his cheekbone. I felt it crack against my knuckles bulging out of my fist and saw him stagger back away from me.

But he would get no mercy from me. That wasn't what I was here for.

"Get him!" the crowd screamed as the guy cowered, hanging his head to protect his busted face.

That wouldn't help him, though. Not with me. I knew what my role was. I knew why all these people had come here tonight, and it wasn't to see mercy. Mercy was for suckers. Fuck mercy.

They wanted blood and pain, and blood and pain is what they'd get.

I walked toward him as a feeling of complete calm came over me. All the noise of the crowd around us faded away until all I heard were the words I told myself every time I stood to fight.

It's you or him. Nothing more. Either you win or he does, but if you lose, you'll have nothing.

He looked up and I saw the pleading in his eyes. I'd seen it fifteen times before. No matter how big and tough they'd been in the beginning, each one ended up giving me that same sad look that said they wanted me to be someone other than who they'd heard I was.

Someone other than who I had to be.

Maybe they fought for some reason that had nothing to do with their very survival. Maybe they thought it would be fun, or it would make them feel tough. Maybe they thought they had something to prove to some girl. Whatever their reasons for agreeing to fight, they weren't why I fought.

For me, every win put me one step closer to being free. I didn't fight for shits and giggles or because I wanted to impress some skirt. I fought for the chance that one day I would never have to step foot in this fucking shithole place again. I fought because deep in the back of my mind there existed the tiniest dream that one day I'd be normal and have a normal life.

That one day I wouldn't have to be the man I'd been forced to become in this fight.

I knew his weak spots and attacked them. My fists pummeled his face, and no matter how hard he tried to shield himself from the blows, it was no use. Over and over, I hit him until that pretty face of his looked like mangled hamburger. Blood, flesh, and bone mixed to make a horror show. The nose that had been so straight just a few minutes before now pointed down toward his mouth like some deranged compass.

As I stood up to my full height, I heard the crowd cheering, as if I'd done something worthy of praise. A man lay in a crumpled heap at my feet, defeated and broken, and these fuckers were thrilled about it.

Looking around, I saw some clapping and others pumping their fists in the air as my win filled them with some kind of messed up happiness. Who was I kidding? What it filled was their wallets. That's why they were so happy.

Floyd raised my right arm in the air to the delight of the rabid fans and said in my ear, "That's my boy. You done good, son."

I forced a smile and nodded my head. I wasn't his boy and he wasn't my father. I was his fighter and he was the scumbag who went out to find people for me to fight. Whatever else he thought we were was all in his mind.

He lowered my arm and slapped me on the back. "Go relax. You deserve it. You put on a good show. Just look at the way these people love you!"

I tore my stare from his greasy comb-over and beady eyes and looked over his head to see the people who loved me. Between the booze, the drugs, and the fight, they looked like wild animals.

Who was worse? Them or me?

"RYDER, THERE'S SOMEONE here to talk to you,"
Floyd yelled from the other side of the door.

I didn't want to talk to anyone. All I wanted
to do was sit on my crappy metal folding chair in
this dingy room and hope my shoulder started
feeling better. I'd downed a few shots of Floyd's
whisky about ten minutes ago, but so far, it
hadn't helped ease the pain.

"Not now," I yelled back.

He'd only open the door anyway. I knew that.
It still felt good to let him and whoever the hell
was standing there with him know that I didn't
want to talk.

The door opened a second later and I saw
Floyd and some guy who looked far too well-
dressed to be anywhere near the warehouse on any
night standing in my shitty little room. He had a
vibe that screamed money with his suit, expensive
shoes, and slicked back grey hair that made him
look what my mother used to call stately.

"This is Mr. Robert Erickson," Floyd said as
the man walked into the room like he owned the
place. "I'll leave you two to talk."

I'd never seen Floyd leave a scene that fast. As
he closed the door, I looked at the man who stood

in front of me and saw he was studying me as much as I was him. Not that I was all too curious about what he wanted. People dressed like he was coming into my world never brought anything good with them.

Never.

The intruder looked around the cinder block room I called mine and then looked down at me. "Ryder, as our mutual friend Floyd said, my name is Robert Erickson. Do you know who I am?"

Shaking my head, I shrugged. "Nope. Should I?"

His dark eyebrows drew in like angry black slashes and his eyes narrowed to slits, much like the way the guy I just beat to a pulp had looked at the beginning of our fight. "I'm the man who runs this show. You are sitting in my warehouse and fighting in my stable. So yes, maybe you should know who I am."

As much as I knew he thought I should be impressed by this, I wasn't. Folding my arms across my chest, I said, "Oh yeah? Nice to meet the big boss then. I hope you bet on me tonight."

His eyes opened wider as the corners of his mouth inched up into what reminded me of how a crocodile looked right before he ate his prey. "You're pretty sure of yourself, aren't you?"

I looked up at the ceiling for a moment,

unsure how I should answer that. Fuck yeah, I was sure of myself. I may not have been wearing a thousand dollar suit and fine leather shoes like him, but I had gifts of my own that had made me a winner sixteen times already.

Pursing my lips, I shrugged again. "I haven't lost yet. Come see me when I do and I'll tell you how cocky I'm feeling then."

His crocodile smile spread even wider across his face. Nodding, he said, "I'll remember that. For now, I'm here to tell you I've bought your contract from Floyd. So now you work for only me."

The words hit me like a fist to the face. I didn't have a contract with Floyd or anyone else. I fought to pay off money I owed him, and when that debt was paid off, I'd get to leave this shithole world of fighting. Now all that seemed like a pipe dream this fucker had dashed to pieces.

I stood from my rusted metal chair and stared at Robert Erickson. "What does that mean?"

Nearly the same height, he met my gaze with one so intense I thought about taking a step back. When he spoke, it sounded like his voice came from somewhere dark.

"It means I own you now. You fight for me and I expect you to win like you always have."

Left unsaid was the implicit threat that hung

off every word. If you lose, you'll suffer. The only question was how.

My mind spun at the news that all I'd planned, all I'd worked for, was gone now. "So I guess my deal with Floyd to be released from fighting when I paid off what I owed him is gone too?"

"Yes."

"And if I don't agree to this new deal?" I asked, silently gauging my chances of not only getting past him but finding some way of surviving after I got away. He was big, and I had a sneaking suspicion even bigger guys stood outside waiting for him.

Robert Erickson looked like the type of man who got what he wanted, one way or another, whether the other person involved wanted it or not.

"You have no say in it, but let me assure you that you want to fight for me. For now, let's get you to your place so you can pack your things."

He turned to open the door as I explained this room was my place. "No need to go anywhere. You're already in it."

Erickson slowly looked back at me with confusion written all over his face. "You live here?"

I nodded. "Yeah. Short commute time to

work and everything I need within arm's reach. What more could a guy ask for?"

Closing the door, he turned to face me. "How old are you?"

"Eighteen."

"And you live here, in my warehouse where Floyd holds fights for me?" he asked as he looked around my room again, this time with a look of disgust like the fact made him sick.

"Yep. Better than the street or jail. I might not get three hots, but I got a cot and a shower."

My answer didn't make the sickened expression leave his face, but he nodded anyway. "Well, gather your things. It's time to go."

I opened my mouth to ask where, but he walked out and left me standing there in that room I'd lived in for the past three months. As I stuffed the few clothes I owned, deodorant, and my toothbrush into a duffel bag, I thought wherever I was going had to be better than this place.

WE PULLED UP to a massive black gate between two even bigger rows of hedges and stopped momentarily as the driver got the go ahead to drive onto the property. I couldn't help but stare out the window as we drove up the long driveway past some kind of fountain that looked like something the Greek gods might swim in and a bunch of smaller hedges than the ones out front that looked like the gardener had cut them all into bird shapes. Robert Erickson was even richer than I'd first thought. Only insanely wealthy people lived in places like this.

The car stopped in front of a house so big I couldn't see all of it as I looked out the car window. Erickson tapped me on the arm as I stared out at the mansion and said, "Welcome home."

Home? This couldn't be my home. Instantly, the thought of what I'd have to do to live in a place like this raced through my mind. Fighting in The Pit wasn't going to be enough to live in a house like the one I saw in front of me.

I opened the car door and stepped out onto a stone driveway as I gaped at the house, which was even more impressive without the tinting of the car window getting in my way. Huge white columns towered above us to the second story of the gold colored home, and a glass front door so enormous I'd never seen one so big stood behind them.

"Follow me," was all Erickson said as he led the way to those doors. I couldn't imagine what waited inside after an outside this incredible.

I did as he ordered and caught up to him as he

walked into an entryway so big the sound of our shoes hitting the white marble tile on the floor echoed off the matching marble tiled walls. He strode through like nothing around us was special toward the most spectacular curved wrought iron staircase I'd ever seen.

Not that I had seen many curved staircases with wrought iron in my life. I think I'd seen either a grand total of two times in a magazine some girl had in English class one time. I really didn't have much interest in reading architectural magazines, but she did and since I wanted to get in her pants, I sat next to her after school as she told me all about her dreams of having a huge house with a curved staircase and a wrought iron railing one day.

She would have loved Erickson's place. For me, it made me feel small, something very few people or things had achieved in a long time. Not small, actually. More like insignificant.

As my head swiveled left and right to look at the artwork on the walls, Robert said, "Come in here to my office. I want you to meet some people."

My hand clutched the handle of my duffel bag tightly in my palm. Meet some people? I didn't even look like they'd let me on the property to be the goddamned gardener who made hedges into animal shapes and now he wanted to introduce me to some people?

That feeling of insignificance morphed into one of pure discomfort. I didn't belong there, no matter how much he wanted to parade me through the place, and whoever he wanted me to meet would know that as sure as I did.

He led me into his office, a room even bigger than the entryway and as dark as that was light. This room had dark green walls the color of a pool table and a dark wood floor. Floor to ceiling bookcases held books with names I'd never heard of and sculptures I guessed cost more than my life was worth.

"Wait here. I'll be right back," he announced before leaving as I continued to look around in awe.

Seconds later, he came back with two females and ordered them into his office. Neither one looked like him, but something about the way they acted told me they weren't servants or people he'd just basically bought, like me.

They stopped dead at the sight of me standing there in my old gym pants and black t-shirt and the one I figured was older spun around to look at him in disgust.

"Who is this?"

"Girls, this is Ryder. He's going to be living

here, so treat him like family."

Robert's proclamation infuriated her, and she shook her head angrily. "What, like a brother? You go out one night and get us a brother? Is that how it goes, Dad?"

He ignored her outburst and turned his two daughters to face me. "Ryder, the one who can't stop talking is Janelle. The other one is Serena."

"Hi," I mumbled, unsure if I should say anything.

They both stood staring at me like I was some foreign thing that needed to be removed and fast. The one named Janelle had short dark brown hair, and although I couldn't be sure since her eyes were flashing so much hatred, I thought they were brown too. Thin, she wore jeans and a tight blue shirt and heels that gave her at least three inches on her normal height.

The other one, Serena, had lighter brown hair that fell to below her shoulders in soft waves that reminded me of what mermaids looked like. Dressed in jean shorts and a white t-shirt that both showed off her tan and toned body, she stood barefoot next to her father and stared at me with big brown eyes that didn't have hatred but something else in them.

Disappointment?

As Janelle returned to complaining about my

very existence, I heard Serena say in a pained voice, "You said you knew where she was. You promised you'd find her this time. Where is she?"

I imagined that's what that guy with the pleading eyes would have sounded like if he begged me not to beat the shit out of him. The way she said those words made my chest hurt, and I didn't even know who she was talking about.

But Robert was unmoved by her pleading. Waving off her questions, he said, "Maybe next time, honey. For now, I want you two to welcome Ryder to our home."

He put his arms around both of them, but Janelle slipped out of his hold and stormed off without another word. I didn't have to guess how she felt about me. Serena said nothing more about what was obviously so important to her and simply looked at me with that pleading in her eyes that hadn't worked on her father.

With a nudge from him, she finally said, "Welcome to our home. I hope you like it here."

And with that, she quietly left without another word to her father about whoever she wanted him to find.

Robert walked behind his desk and sat down in his chair as I watched her walk away, her sagging shoulders signaling how defeated she felt. Clearly, it didn't affect her father at all.

"They'll get used to you. Janelle is a little temperamental, but I guess that's to be expected from a girl, even one her age. She's a lot like me, though, so at least she has that going for her. Serena is the polar opposite. She's like her mother. Don't worry about her. She'll take to you like every stray she brings home."

Not that I didn't know I looked like some stray dog compared to them, but the way he said it brought the reality home for sure. In a hurry to get out of there and to wherever he kept the strays he brought home, I said, "Well, if you can just point me in the direction of where you want me to go, I'll get out of your hair."

He shook his head as that crocodile smile spread across his face again. "Not yet. First, I want you to know what I expect of you. So sit down and relax."

Dropping my duffel bag, I sat down in a chair in front of his desk as he'd ordered and listened to hear just what this whole arrangement would involve.

He steepled his fingers in front of him and began. "You'll continue to fight as you did tonight. As I said before, I expect you to continue to win. When you do, you'll get paid, despite the fact that you won't need money as long as you live here."

"I won't need money?" I asked, confused what kind of world this guy lived in that didn't require cash.

Lifting his chin, he shook his head. "No, you won't. Your room and board, along with all the food you want and clothes you need, will be provided. I have a state of the art workout center you're to use to make sure you're in the best shape possible. So you see, you won't need money."

I didn't know if I should question this whole situation that sounded too good to be true, but I asked, "And if I don't win a fight?"

His face grew dark. "Let's cross that bridge when we come to it. For now, I have very few rules, other than you performing in fights like I've seen. No drugs and no romantic attachments. I don't care who you fuck, but don't get involved. I remember being your age, so I don't expect you to live like a monk, but no relationships."

I wasn't a fan of having so much of my life dictated, but assuming I got a room even as big as a broom closet on his estate, maybe it wouldn't be too much of a tradeoff. I wasn't exactly looking for a relationship anyway and I didn't do drugs. Hoping he wasn't about to announce that I had to double as a stable boy or something like that, I smiled.

"Okay. I can live with those."

"And you aren't to tell anyone here what you do. Is that clear?"

"Sure. But if I'm not here as a fighter, what am I supposed to say if someone asks?"

"They won't," he said with a confidence I guessed came from being the boss.

"Got it."

"Good. I'll have my housekeeper take you to your room. For now, you'll have the spare bedroom on this floor."

A short, dark haired woman he called Josephine appeared a few seconds later, so I stood from my chair and grabbed my duffel bag to go with her. I felt like there were a lot more questions I should ask Robert, but he didn't seem interested in talking anymore and picked up the phone to call someone, so I smiled again and moved to leave.

Just before I reached the door, he said, "Oh, Ryder, one more thing."

There it was. The one thing that would make this whole situation unbearable. I slowly turned around and waited for the other shoe to drop.

"Don't even think of doing anything with either of the girls. In that respect, I do care who you fuck."

I thought back to how much Janelle hated me already and easily put the idea of fucking her out of my mind. And Serena? I wasn't sure if she was even legal, and I didn't need that dogging me. An angry father was one thing, but prison was an entirely different story.

She was beautiful, though. There was something about her I could definitely like, if things were different. But no matter how beautiful she was, I wasn't touching that.

"No problem," I answered with confidence, hoping that was the worst thing about living at Erickson's house.

If it was, this would be the best thing to ever happen to me, even if it meant I had to keep fighting. Maybe freedom wasn't all it was cracked up to be anyway.

**LOOK FOR THE CORRUPTED LOVE
TRILOGY TODAY!
AVAILABLE AT ALL MAJOR RETAILERS**

About the Author

K.M. Scott writes contemporary romance stories of sexy, intense, and unforgettable love. A New York Times and USA Today bestselling author, she's been in love with romance since reading her first romance novel in junior high (she was a very curious girl!). Under her Gabrielle Bisset name, she writes erotic paranormal and historical romance. She lives in Pennsylvania with a herd of animals and when she's not writing can be found reading or feeding her TV addiction.

Be sure to visit K.M.'s Facebook page at **facebook.com/kmscottauthor** for all the latest on her books, along with giveaways and other goodies! And to hear all the news on K.M. Scott books first, sign up for her newsletter today and be sure to visit her website at **www.kmscottbooks.com**.

Books by K.M. Scott:

If I Dream (Corrupted Love #1)
If You Fight (Corrupted Love #2)
If We Fall (Corrupted Love #3)

Crash Into Me (Heart of Stone #1)
Fall Into Me (Heart of Stone #2)
Give In To Me (Heart of Stone #3)
Heart of Stone Volume One Box Set
Ever After (Heart of Stone #4)
A Heart of Stone Christmas (Heart of Stone #5)
Unforgettable (Heart of Stone #6)
Unbreakable (Heart of Stone #7)
Heart of Stone Volume Two Box Set

Temptation (Club X #1)
Surrender (Club X #2)
Possession (Club X #3)
Satisfaction (Club X #4)
Acceptance (Club X #5)
The Complete Club X Series Box Set

Crave (Addicted To You #1)
Adore (Addicted To You #2)
Shatter (Addicted To You #3)
Claim (Addicted To You #4)

K.M.'S BOOKS ARE IN AUDIOBOOK TOO!

Books by Gabrielle Bisset:

Vampire Dreams Revamped (A Sons of Navarus Prequel)
Blood Avenged (Sons of Navarus #1)
Blood Betrayed (Sons of Navarus #2)
Longing (A Sons of Navarus Short Story)
Blood Spirit (Sons of Navarus #3)
The Deepest Cut (A Sons of Navarus Short Story)
Blood Prophecy (Sons of Navarus #4)
Blood Craving (Sons of Navarus #5)
Blood Eclipse (Sons of Navarus #6)
The Sons of Navarus Box Set #1
The Sons of Navarus Box Set #2

Stolen Destiny (Destined Ones Duology #1)
Destiny Redeemed (Destined Ones Duology #2)

Love's Master
Masquerade
The Victorian Erotic Romance Trilogy